The H   House

Shawn C. McLain

The Grey Girl, Book One
The Haunting of Sterben House

Copyright 2018 ©Shawn C. McLain
ISBN 978-0-692-19567-3

Cover art created by Colin Richards
Colinrichardsart@facebook.com

For my wife, as always

And in memory of Alex, Weasley, Oliver, and Tasha

To Justine
Enjoy The
Horror

THE DARE

"Go on!" A cold wind rustled the dead leaves. "What? Are you...scared?" a young boy's taunting voice asked.

"I'm not scared. You're stupid," a trembling voice answered as shadows of the trees danced across the dark bricks and blank windows.

"Told you he wouldn't do it." A third, bored voice harrumphed.

Three boy's voices hissed furiously at one another.

The whispered argument ended with "You're so tough, then come in with me."

Silence ensued, followed by "Bet you won't."

The three boys glared at one another. A nod of agreement was made all around. A moment's hesitation before they crept slowly toward the rusting fence, where they paused. Each pointed at another to go first. No one moved. Throwing his hands in the air in frustration, the tallest of the three ducked. Slipping through the hole by the bush that couldn't be seen from the road, they followed one after the other. Back together on the other side, they nodded, grim-faced and determined. Three shadows ran, heads low, through the wild tall grass and weeds. Vines and brushes tugged at their legs. Each step forward felt like someone trying to stop them. Finally they ascended the creaking wooden porch. Footfalls dull and hollow echoed through the aged wood.

"How do we get in?" asked a squeaking whisper.

"Stephanie's brother says there is a loose board over a broken window over here." One of the boys quaked. Wood scraped on battered wood as the board was pushed aside, revealing their way in. Not one of them moved. Again each looked to the others, eyebrows raised expectantly.

Finally, "Come on," the tallest grumbled. One by one, they disappeared through the gap.

Though the wind rustled the leaves outside, the room was silent. The trio stood close together and even closer to the way out. Dust-encrusted cloth-covered furnishings made strange shapes throughout the area. Sparse light from outside illuminated little. A light flashed across the once-elegant front room as one boy produced a small flashlight. Each step forward sent small clouds of dust into the air. The flashlight's weak beam held with a shaking hand led the way as the huddle moved into the hall. Portraits glared down at them from long-dead eyes.

Heavy thumps from above ceased all movement and breathing. The flashlight slowly pointed up at the ceiling. A shower of dust caught the beam. "Probably just a homeless guy," whispered an unconvinced voice. The rhythmic thumps continued like footsteps. The sound seemed to move, getting farther away as, silently, they listened. The light followed the progress of dust fall till it shone on the darkness where the staircase disappeared onto the second floor. Shuffling as one, the boys found themselves staring, dry-mouthed and shaking, from the bottom of the grand staircase.

A voice screamed from behind them: "*Get out!*" The light flickered and flashed, spinning to reveal a face of terror, translucent and ghastly. The flashlight rolled across the floor, its rattle drowned by the screams of the boys and the thundering of their feet. One of the retreating boys caught something out of the corner of his eye. The sheer horror of it caused him to pause. Something hideous lumbered down the stairs. The boy's mouth opened into a scream when a hand

2

grabbed his collar. The loose board flew across the porch out into the overgrown lawn. Glass shattered as one head was not ducked low enough. Two went through the hole in the fence while the last one hurdled over. Several minutes later, near the well-lit porch of one boy, a pact was made.

The three swore never to tell anyone what they had seen that night. They also swore, silently to themselves as they parted, to never go near the old Sterben Hall ever again.

1932

Edgar Davies drove along the dusty country lane in the crisp fall sunshine. He had been traveling for a little while. The distance of home from town annoyed him. He barely noticed the morning dew still glistening on the tall grass along the side of the road. He felt nothing but contempt for the smaller farms and the people who lived in them as he passed. Cresting a hill, he spied a young woman walking alone, her school books held tightly against her gray wool coat. Edgar slowed as he approached, taking in her gray suede shoes, the nice-fitting coat, and the green ribbon in her hair. He slowed more, coming level to her. She glanced at the truck but kept walking. Edgar leaned over, rolling down the window with some difficulty. Trying to keep pace with her, he leaned across the seat. His grip on the wheel caused him to swerve toward the girl. She stutter-stepped sideways to avoid collision. Frowning, she glared into the cab and kept walking, increasing her pace.

Edgar cursed the mistake. "Hey," he called. "You're the Miller girl, right?" She nodded but kept walking, head down, not looking in his direction. "I'm Edgar Davies," he said proudly, waiting for recognition. "You know, of the Sterben Davieses," he stated pompously. Now it was his turn to frown. She simply nodded but kept walking. Edgar decided to change tact. "Hey! Karen, right? How 'bout I give you a ride? It is cold out there."

Finally she paused slightly. "My name is Chloe," she corrected as she continued forward. "Thank you for the offer, but I prefer to walk." Her reply was polite but firm. She had heard the stories about Edgar and his offers. Chloe did not wish to find out their validity.

4

Edgar's fist balled on the seat; anger blazed in his eyes. The engine revved; the wheels turned then screeched to a halt. Chloe, shocked, stumbled back off the curb in fear. The anger on his face and the fear on hers stared at each other. Chloe held her breath. A tear began to form in the corner of her eye. Edgar enjoyed the fear he had caused. A smile appeared on his face. He shrugged as if nothing had happened. "Suit yourself. Have a fine day, Chloe Miller."

"You as well, Mr. Davies." She nodded, trying to smile back. The truck sped away, leaving Chloe breathing hard with relief as she swiped at the tear that still threatened to fall. She'd heard about a girl from school who had accepted a ride from Edgar. He had made many advances and many demands, even threatening to impugn her character if she did not do what he asked. She stopped, calming her breathing. Shaking off the shiver that had nothing to do with the cold, she continued on her way, pondering what she should tell her friends.

The smile slid from Edgar's face as he drove away, replaced by the ugly scowl he wore whenever he thought about this place. Slamming a fist onto the steering wheel, he shouted at the empty road ahead. "Who does she think she is?" A squirrel scurried from the brush. Edgar sped up. The creature flew back to safety. "Damn it. Who cares? She's just a silly farm girl." Edgar often thought this way. His family owned half the county. "She should have been flattered I stopped to offer her a ride," he grumbled. He'd had enough of the simple girls of this town. Ever since they had moved here, buying the Sterben estate, the people of the town had been crass and standoffish. "It's pathetic how they envy the wealthy and powerful." His knuckles were white on the wheel; red rimmed his vision as he cursed Chloe and the town. Women back in the city had finally started to take notice when his family had achieved their high status. They never would have refused his offer. He knew none had refused his brother, so why would they refuse him? Not that he had had the guts to ask when he lived there. There were so many other distractions, he assured himself. "But now," he frowned, "we live here."

As soon as Chloe arrived, she asked her friend, Charlie, if she should say anything to the teacher. His reply was noncommittal. The Davies were very influential as well as a large employer. The day wore on, and Chloe tried to put the morning further and further from her mind. By lunch it was simply an interaction with creepy Edgar that she shared with her friends. By the time the final bell rang, no one thought any more about it. She laughed as her friends told her to not accept rides from "strange" men. As the group walking home together from the school dwindled and the houses became sparser, the humor evaporated, becoming as bare as the landscape. Darkness was coming fast with the overcast skies. The temperature had fallen throughout the day. With the last goodbye said several minutes earlier in her travel, it was not the cold that caused Chloe to wrap her coat tighter while quickening her pace but the low growl of an engine.

Edgar's day was spent as many of his days were. He arrived in town to oversee operations at his father's mill. Being the supervisor meant sitting in his office drinking coffee till noon, smoking with his favorite slacker employees, then a few card games and drinking whiskey after 2:00 p.m. Today Edgar was bored and angry. His afternoon had not gone according to routine. There had been problems that needed to be addressed, employees that needed managing, and paperwork to be done. Through it all, the thought of the girl from the morning kept interfering. By four o'clock, the bottle held no more than a swallow, and he'd had enough of work. He decided to sneak out for the day. Announcing he had to concentrate on work, he slammed his door. The staff barely registered the outburst other than to grumble doubts of his "working." Feeling he had fooled them, he left through the window.

Cursing the empty fields, the dirt roads, and the mill, Edgar began the only pastime he felt was open to him, drinking. His family had visited this tiny town a few times in the past. His brother had always liked the Sterben Hall. Edgar never understood why, but as his family's fortunes grew, that of the Holt family declined. Then came the collapse. The Holts lost almost everything through a scandalous scheme that bankrupted the Mill. Many people lost their jobs and would have lost their homes if Edgar's family had not swooped in and bought the mill and the Sterben Hall, saving the town. "So that little hussy owes me her very existence," Edgar grumbled as he tossed an empty bottle out the window.

Summer Job

The summer after Alex Holt's senior year of high school
could have been better. It was the first summer since his
mother had passed away. She had died just as the family
business was starting to take off. Between the medical bills and
the need for help with the company, Alex had started working
with his father and brother. They owned a restoration and
general contracting business: Holt and Sons Construction and
Restoration. Alex's father, Arthur Holt, and Alex's brother,
Aaron, had been the company's two employees since Aaron had
graduated as an electrician from trade school. Together they
had built up a nice reputation, a reputation that was finally
overshadowing the old stories about the family. How the once
proud Holt family had lost their fortune and standing in a
community with hints at witchcraft and deals with the devil.
Even after nearly a hundred years, there were still some older
folks who whispered and pointed when his family appeared in
town. Some even went so far as to blame the old rumors for his
mother's cancer. Alex never listened to what he called
"superstitious old fools," as there was another family name in
town with an even worse reputation.

Even with his dislike for the small-mindedness and his
desire to escape, he had to admit the town had undergone a
renaissance lately. For reasons Alex couldn't comprehend,
people from the city were investing in the area. They found the
commute was easy and the property inexpensive. Many people
were buying up the larger old houses and returning them from
apartments and rentals back to the stately grandeur they'd once
had. This held a twofold effect for the Holt's business. All the

houses needed work, and no one cared about rumors from years ago. The only reputation they cared about was the current one of doing excellent and fast work.

Even though Alex's desire was to get out and see what else life could have in store, as the summer drew to a close, he decided against college. There was so much work to do that he made the decision to stay home, for maybe another year, to continue helping his father and brother. This was nothing new. For as long as he could remember, he would make sacrifices to help with the family business. This included hanging out after school, sports, weekends, and most socializing. This was fine with Alex, as he didn't really fit in at school or in town either. This was a huge departure from his father and brother, both well liked in the community. Their hard work brought more people to the town, and more people brought more business.

Today Alex spent the morning attempting to keep his anxiety to himself. They had been waiting all morning for news on a big project. If Aaron was as uptight, he wasn't saying anything. As they loaded up the work van, they waited in silence for their father to return. Both men froze. Their eyes locked, hearing the bell over the door of the office.

"It's Pops," Aaron whispered.

Alex spun to look. "I can't tell. What do you think?"

Aaron's frown told Alex he couldn't tell their father's feelings either. He had gone out to the public auction early that morning. The auction was for the old mansion on the outskirts of town. The place had been empty for years. The previous owners had never been to it. People in town said it was tax write-off for them. Apparently, it hadn't worked, as the place was foreclosed. The owners before them had left the place in the middle of the night after only a few months, putting it up for sale. Albert's father had made an attempt to buy it then and a couple of times after but could never afford it.

Approaching the office, Alex and Aaron pushed and hissed at each other, pointing and threatening. At the door Alex cleared his throat. "Well, Dad? How did it go?" he asked in a would-be casual tone.

"Load up the gear, boys; we have work to do," Arthur grumbled. Alex and Aaron exchanged disappointed looks. Aaron nodded. At the cue Alex adopted a positive tone.

"Ah, well, Pops, not a big deal. I'm sure the place will be back on the market in a couple of years."

"Or months even," Aaron added hopefully.

Arthur watched his boys for a few moments. "We take possession of the Sterben house at the end of the month." The mood shifted instantly. The slapping of high-fives and the shouts forced Arthur's voice to rise. "Until then we still have other projects to finish up. Get it in gear!"

"Oh man, if Gramps was still here, he would be so stoked!" Alex shouted.

"Yeah, Dad was obsessed with that place and not just because—" Arthur's phone rang. "Yes, we are on our way, Mrs. Thayer." Hanging up, he called out, "Thayer's all mad about the mess you boys left. Let's get over there and finish up."

"Mess!" Alex cried. "We left a box of tools in the corner behind the flooring." Alex felt his blood pressure rising. "Come on, Dad, we left the place cleaner than when we arrived."

Arthur waved a hand over his shoulder. "Yeah, yeah, let's just get this done."

"Yeah, so we don't have to deal with the old broad anymore," Aaron whispered to his brother. Alex, frowning, nodded his agreement.

<u>1990</u>

"I don't like it here. I want to go back to Philadelphia," young Emily Stewart complained to her parents. Her mother ignored her, taking stock of the furnishings in the old manor house they had just purchased.

"We might be able to sell some of this old junk." Frowning, she turned glaring at the antiques as if they had insulted her. "Maybe recoup some of our wasted money," Mrs. Stewart grumbled.

"This place is great. We got a good deal on it. Just a few renovations and we'll have an awesome bed-and-breakfast." The gleeful voice seemed out of place against the frowning faces. "Besides we can use some of this stuff. I mean it is period correct for the house." Mr. Stewart smiled, pulling dusty sheet after dusty sheet from the old furniture. "Come on, Em, you're going to have a great time here." He didn't notice the looks on his wife's and daughter's faces, looks that said he was the only one enjoying the experience.

A thundering pounding from above turned all three faces to the ceiling.

"It sounds like somebody stomping around upstairs," Emily whispered. Her fear caused her to grip her stuffed bunny closer.

"Must be the old plumbing." Mr. Stewart frowned. "That is gonna be costly.

He sighed. "There's more of my money gone."

"Honey, this was your dream too."

"This was never my dream!"

Emily slowly disappeared as her parents' voices rose like they always did when it came to money or this house. She paused at the foot of the staircase. Cold seeped down from

11

above. Emily shivered as she backed away. She wandered down the detritus-strewn hall to the kitchen. Cabinet doors hung wide, revealing empty shelves or a few cracked dishes. The floor was strewn with shattered plates. Emily frowned. "Why can't people leave stuff alone? There is no reason to destroy this stuff," she stated, picking up half a plate to examine the wheat pattern on it. "Bet it was a bunch of stupid teenagers," she explained to the plush rabbit.

"It wasn't," whispered a voice behind Emily.

The shard clattered to the floor. "Who's there?" Emily's eyes searched the corners of the room. She was alone. She backed quickly into the hall. Her parents' argument was reaching new decibels. Shaking the voice from her head, she stared at her bunny. "Must have been them fighting." Deciding on the other direction, Emily made her way into the large banquet room. More dishes lay scattered and broken on the table and floors. The centerpiece was dead and dry. Dust lay thick on everything.

Something, moving maybe, caught her attention through a door at the end of the room. "Hello?" Emily called, taking a step forward. Light was spilling from the inch or two between the door and the frame. She was sure a shadow passed by. Emily rolled her shoulders, moved her head from side to side, as she had seen her father do when he was determined to do something. She pushed on the door, but it resisted. Frowning, she pushed harder. Rusty hinges broke free. Creaking loudly, the door unveiled a large conservatory. All the plants were brown, tan, and brittle. The glass was filthy, letting in muted light. Several statues and busts littered the room. Movement in the corner of her eye caught her attention. There was someone standing there.

Emily was stunned to see a very pretty young woman standing partway behind one of the old busts. She was looking away from Emily as if scared of her. The girl wore a long gray-wool coat even though it was very warm in the room. Emily saw the woman was missing a shoe, but that wasn't the only thing odd about her. There was something less about the woman. Her face seemed kind yet sad. A trick of the light. That must have been it. That was what caused Emily to see horrors on the girl's face. Such pain, it caused her to look away. When she looked again, it was the pretty face again.

"Hello?" Emily questioned. The young woman moved out of hiding. She looked up to face her as if just noticing her.

"You shouldn't be here," the woman whispered.

"Um, no, it is you that shouldn't be here," Emily replied, placing her hands on her hips. The bunny swinging by a leg held tight. "My parents bought this place; it is ours now."

"No, it isn't. He will not like you here," was the whispered reply; the woman was looking up toward the house's second floor. Emily turned to follow the gaze.

"Who won't...?" When Emily turned back, the woman was gone. She searched the conservatory but couldn't figure out where the woman had gone. Emily's mother calling returned her to the front room. Emily's father was not there. The tears on her mother's face were barely dry, but the anger was still in her eyes.

"Where is Dad?" Emily quietly asked.

"Upstairs to investigate the horrid plumbing or something else wasteful," Mrs. Stewart grumbled.

"I met a lady in the garden room," Emily stated.

"That's nice. Does she want to buy this pit?"

"She said a man wouldn't like what Dad is doing here."

"Well, they aren't the only ones." Mrs. Stewart growled, pulling a heavily dusty cloth free from a statue. "How many of these damn things are in this place?" she shouted.

A howling cry spread from the back of the house to the front parlor. It seemed to come from the upstairs, gaining in hatred as it spread. Emily covered her ears, crouching under a table. Her mother stood with her hands on her hips, as Emily had done, staring up at the sound. "What the hell has your stupid father done this time?"

Mr. Stewart threw open the front door. "What the hell is that?" he called over the din. Mrs. Stewart spun in shock to see him enter.

"What did you do?" she demanded.

"Me? I've been outside this whole time!" The smell of cigarettes followed him in. The sound faded. Emily left as a fresh fight began about the sound and the smoking.

Emily couldn't remember a worse time in her life. Over the next few weeks, the troubles and tensions grew. She would watch her mother or father move a piece of furniture. Within hours it was back in its original place. The person who moved it would blame the other or Emily. The shouting would start all over again. If they decided to get rid of something, Emily's father would swear and struggle to get it out of the house. Several pieces could not be taken through the doors. Emily's mother would scream about her father not wanting to get rid of anything. They would fight and fight about how he wasn't trying hard enough while he complained she did nothing to help, only nag. When he finally did get something out of the house to the car, then the car wouldn't start. This, of course, led to another scream fest, as Emily put it. With all of the troubles with cleaning and tensions, little work was actually getting done. The only thing that Emily could see had changed was much of the dust and many of the broken items had been able to be removed. What was still there was anything that was whole. It sat scattered in the rooms or on the front porch.

Trying to avoid her angry parents, Emily spent more and more time alone. She had tried many times to find the woman in the conservatory but with minimal results. She would catch a glimpse or see her watching from the halls. Emily had given up trying to tell her parents about the girl. They never listened. The few times Emily was able to speak to the woman, it was always the same: *Leave the house before it is too late. Leave before he gets angry.* In the end Emily gave up on trying to make friends with her. She never could even get the woman's name. On top of that, her parents thought it was only an imaginary friend.

One afternoon, Mr. Stewart was on the front porch smoking and seething about the most recent exchange with his wife. Mrs. Stewart, for her part, was curled up in one of the ornate chairs she wanted desperately to get rid of. Her temper still burned as she finishing a second bottle of wine. Avoiding the smells of cigarettes and wine, Emily was miserably pushing an old metal car she had found in one of the bedrooms around. Her hand shook over the toy. Dust rained down on her as the heavy thumping above started. Emily tried to ignore the sounds until the howl started. The toy forgotten, Emily ran from the room. She collided with her father at the bottom of the stairs. Mrs. Stewart was in the doorway of the sitting room ten feet away. Emily was being helped up by her father; the stink of smoke burned Emily's nose. It was worse than normal. It smelled of rotten eggs and something far worse.

On her feet, she ignored her father's apologies. Emily was staring at her mother. Seeing his daughter's distraction, he turned to his wife. Mrs. Stewart was standing straight-backed, wide-eyed with a shaking finger pointed behind Emily. Emily turned slowly to see the young woman standing there. It was then that Emily noticed she could see through her. The girl's head hung down; the look on her face was so sad it made Emily want to cry. Beside her, Emily could feel her father shaking and sputtering. His head swiveled from the girl to his wife and back again. The look in his eyes was begging this to be a joke.

"You must leave. He is coming," whispered the woman.

"What the hell is that?" Mr. Stewart cried, grabbing Emily as he rushed to his wife. Emily grabbed her mother's arm, trying to pull her to the front door. Mrs. Stewart couldn't or wouldn't move. The ghost stood unmoving, head still down, repeating her warning.

"Go now before it is too late. He is angry." The young woman's sad eye turned to the hall. She vanished as another howl followed by a cold wind and heavy footfalls thundered from above.

A half-empty wine bottle shattered. Mrs. Stewart was screaming. Her cries mixed with Mr. Stewart's. Emily shut her eyes tight. At the top of the stairs stood hell itself. Eyes of pure hatred blazed out of white flesh pulled tightly over a skull that broke through along the sharp cheeks. A bony finger pointed out of a filthy rotted sleeve at the huddled family.

"*Get out!*" boomed the horror.

Emily was in her father's arms. Her mother was still screaming. Her father was yelling and pulling his wife with him. She threw off his arm and flew through the door. In a blur they were outside. Three car doors slammed. The front door stood wide open. Down the stairs they could see a cloud of black descending, the face from the top visible through the smoke. The car burst to life. Emily found herself sliding around in the backseat. She turned to take a last look at the house, a house she would never set foot in again. In a window in the conservatory, she saw a figure standing. Emily shut her eyes tightly, willing the vision to go away.

The family returned to Philadelphia where the divorce was final, the house was sold, and Emily spent many years in therapy trying to convince herself it had never happened.

<u>1932</u>

Edgar felt himself sinking into the driver's seat, becoming numb as the whiskey flowed over his tongue and burned his throat. The warmth spread through his body while his head felt that familiar disconnect. After a while, the pleasing sensations gave way as they always did to darker thoughts. The amber liquid changed from a comfort to the fuel for his anger. It brought back the same needling questions: *Why am I the one stuck with all the lousy jobs while my stinking younger brother runs the main office with father?* He stewed, sometimes hating his brother's face. Another few drinks replaced the thoughts with just the emotions.

Blurred vision and angry depression caused Edgar to pay little attention to where he was going. The fields and dirt roads melted into one long stream of nothing. He was starting to creep into the oblivion that was always the goal at the end of the bottle. He was almost there when he recognized the gray-wool coat up ahead. Black tunnels crept into his vision, a vision that was tinged with red and already blurring into double. "It's her fault!" he slurred, trying to point to her; his hand slipped across the wheel before falling onto the seat in an attempt to keep himself upright. "I mean I wasn't going to hurt her. If she had been a smart girl and just gotten in." His head spun as he tried to focus on her. She separated into two, then three. Squeezing his eyes shut, trying to clear his vision, shaking his head violently. There were still two or three of her in his vision. He growled out his continued anger. "I'm a handsome man, a nice man, a wealthy man. She was just a stupid country girl." The whiskey bottle was at his lips again.

"She doesn't matter," a voice hissed in his ear. "You could do anything you wanted, and no one could do anything to a rich, important man like you."

Edgar slapped the dash. "Damn right I can. I could..." His rant ceased with the heavy thud against the left side of the truck. The brakes locked, the tires screamed in chorus with the scream he didn't realize he had heard.

The world stopped. All Edgar could hear was his own heavy breathing. He was leaning forward, arms up over his head. A pain, dulled by whiskey, throbbed on his forehead. Slowly leaning back in the seat, he noticed only one headlight was aglow. He giggled uneasily as his shaking fingers searched the floor until they found the bottle. He glared at the contents, noting some had spilled. The alcohol burned his throat. A low moan caused the bottle to slip from his lips, letting the amber liquid cascade over his chin falling into his lap. The cold air was a shock, clearing his head slightly as he found himself outside of the cab without knowing how.

The red glow of the taillights outlined a lump on the side of the road. "It's a deer," he slurred. "It's only a deer." A tear slipped from his eye as Edgar crept closer, the panic growing with each step. A cry broke the quiet, sending birds into flight from the field. Edgar fell back onto the ground, kicking uselessly, trying to get back. The lump moved. That was not what sent terror coursing through him. Deer had moved, jumped, and even run off after being hit. This one moaned. With a strangled cry, a hand appeared above the body. It clawed at the gravel. Transfixed with horror, Edgar watched as the hand tried to pull its broken body and legs off the road.

Over the agonizing cries and moans of pain, Edgar was mumbling. "Oh shit, oh god, oh shit!" Gaining his feet, he tried to clear his head. Steadying himself against the rear fender, he took several calming breaths even as the whiskey threatened to come back on him.

The voice was in his ear again. "OK, you've hit deer before; this is no different." Edgar was staring into the bed of the truck. "Just move the corpse off the road, tell father you hit a deer, and get the truck fixed." Shakily, Edgar nodded. "It is going to be all right."

"Pl...please...help...me..." a weak voice called.

WORK TO BE DONE

The busy summer slid into fall. The days were getting shorter while the winds got colder. Dry leaves crunched under heavy tires. Two trucks pulled up to the high fence. Alex frowned at the *No Trespassing* sign, a sign he knew too well was often ignored. He and Aaron had made it to the porch before a car scared them off. The day had already been a long one. It was early afternoon when they arrived. It was later than they had planned after having finally finished a project for a very particular client. Arnold had been happy to call it quits for the day, but his sons had become more and more insistent they start on the old house.

"I still cannot believe you bought this place." Alex whooped as his father cut off the padlock holding the gate shut. Alex's fingers gripped the chain link. He stared through it to the large structure. In the weak afternoon sun, the house looked majestic to him. Standing alone in the middle of a huge, flat lawn, the house looked down on a fountain that was once surrounded by lush gardens. The grounds were overgrown and the house boarded up, but to Alex it was a wonder of brick and ornamental carving. "Man, this place is so awesome."

"Shut up, Alex, and get back in the truck." Aaron called from the van emblazoned with "Holt and Sons Restorations." He sat in the driver's seat, his hands open on the wheel, questioning the delay. "We're all anxious." Several angry glares and gestures flashed between the brothers.

"Come on, Alex, get back in the truck!" Arthur called.

"We all know you are afraid of the haunted house, but we have a job to do!" Aaron called mockingly. True it had been Alex who ran when they had heard the car approach. To this day he claimed it was because he didn't want to get into trouble. Alex gave his older brother the finger as he jumped into the passenger seat of the van, his father already slamming the driver's door shut.

Alex's excitement mounted as the house grew the closer they got. It calmed a bit while they proceeded up the long pothole-riddled drive. He could see the years of neglect in the peeling paint and rotted porch. Then a memory crept up from deep in his mind. A mischievous grin began to grow across his face—knowing his brother had been very scared of the old house when they were younger. When Alex had run away from the "car," Aaron had passed him with little effort. This thought caused him to ask the question generally ignored in the household. "You know the story about the gray girl, right?" he asked.

Arnold did not say anything for most of the ride up. Alex waited for an answer. He hoped he hadn't annoyed his father. Alex was about to either ask again or apologize; he wasn't sure which. His father spoke softly. Alex expected to be told it was nothing but a rumor, a silly story told to scare children. He never expected what he heard next.

"Yeah, I've heard the stories." He shrugged. "Like you kids, I tried to see her." They slowed to navigate a particularly deep hole in the drive. "You know your grandfather always had a theory about her."

"Whoa," Alex cried. "Wait, Granddad knew about her?" Alex tried to digest this information. "How long has she been around?" he wondered aloud gaining a look from his father. Deciding not to annoy his father, Alex asked. "What was his theory?"

Arnold chewed his lip as if trying to decide to continue. "Well, when I was younger, your granddad told me about a girl he went to school with that went missing." He eased the truck to a stop, turned off the ignition, and opened the door. Alex sat stunned for a second. Quickly he joined his father. Aaron had joined them. It felt as if the temperature had dropped several degrees from the fence to the front porch. "He says that on the day the girl disappeared, the old owner of this place..." He gestured to the old stately house before the three men. "...well, he tried to pick her up. Apparently, he tried this with a lot of girls. Sometimes he tried too much." Arnold was working on the front door lock, oblivious to his son's fascination. Aaron was trying to pick up on the conversation. The door swung open with a long low squeal. "Well, Gramps said that her name was Chloe, and she went missing after school." Arthur opened a toolbox Aaron had brought, pulling out a flashlight. "They found skid marks and blood on the road but no body." They stood in the cluttered front room taking in the cobwebs and dust.

"So why did Granddad think that what's-his-face had something to do with it?" Alex asked. Aaron pushed past him with a grumble. Alex threw some fallen plaster at his brother, earning him some flying at him in return.

Ignoring the salvos between his boys, he continued: "Well, like I said, they found skid marks and blood and the guy." Arnold was busy replacing the locks on the front door. "Edgar, that was his name, or Edmond, whatever." He shrugged. "Well, he claimed he had hit a dear; see his truck was smashed up on one side."

"This floor seems OK; boards still on most of the windows." Aaron interrupted, smacking a dusty hand on Alex's face. "We got an overgrown greenhouse out back that looks in decent shape. Might need to come down if it is too much work to clean up." Alex pushed Aaron.

"It's a conservatory," Alex corrected. Aaron spared him his best *whatever* look. Alex rolled his eyes in return. "So, this Ed dude had a smashed truck, and a girl is missing, huh? Why didn't the cops arrest him?" Alex inquired. Behind him he could feel Aaron aping him. Ignoring Aaron's continued mocking, he waited for an answer.

"Check upstairs for water damage," Arnold replied, dusting his hands off from finishing with the door. "We'll start setting up the work lights."

"Come on, Dad," Alex complained as he left to retrieve the lights and generator. He nearly ran to the truck, hastily gathered the equipment, then hurried back to the house. "What happened?" he demanded as soon as he was back through the door.

Arthur stared at Alex for a moment as if confused. Suddenly he took up the story again. "The cops did talk to him. He said he was at work when the girl would have been walking." Together they set up one light stand. "Problem is, according to your granddad, no one saw him in the office." Aaron was back now, setting up the second light stand.

"But..." Arnold shrugged. "His brother vouched for him."

"So why did ol' Granddad think this chick didn't just run off?" Aaron asked. Alex was shocked thinking Aaron hadn't been listening. Light filled the room causing Alex to shield his eyes until they adjusted. The harsh work lights sent odd shadows over the walls. Alex was sure something had moved just out of his sight.

"Well, apparently the girl was a real stand-up person—a class act." Arnold adjusted the lights and began pulling dusty cloths from furniture. Cascades of years of neglect streamed through the bright light.

"Wait." Aaron stopped to turn to his father. "If she went to school with Granddad, it was, what, the teens or twenties or something?"

Arnold was inspecting an old sideboard admiring the craftsmanship. "No! How old do you think Granddad was?" His attention turned back to his sons. "It was the early thirties, and she was all set to go to college, Linden Hall even. Women going to college back then were a rarity. He also said she came from a real close family." Arnold was now checking an outlet. "Granddad was positive she didn't run off. Then, of course, there was what he called *evidence*." Arnold smiled to himself as he walked out the door. He had both his sons completely enthralled. Not since they were kids had he held their attention this long. Aaron was now twenty-three and Alex nineteen. They rarely listened to his stories anymore. He could hear their exasperation as he continued to inspect the furniture. After stalling for too long over the antiques, he began collecting his tools.

"Daaad!" the boys cried out in unison. Arthur suppressed a smile. His boys had gone from grown men to ten years old in an instant.

"OK, OK." Arnold held up his hands in defense. "Granddad went to school with this girl and didn't live too far from her. A couple of years after she went missing, he was walking home with a friend who had moved into her old house." He paused for effect. "See, her family left town after she went missing and the father died." It was at this point the house was filled with a terrible mournful cry followed by what sounded like a howl of rage.

"What the hell was that?" Alex asked as he and the other two stared up at the ceiling.

Aaron looked at his father. "I swear the first noise came from the hall."

"Yeah," Alex answered. "But the second one was definitely from upstairs."

"That is weird. I don't have planned to turn the water back on until next week." Arnold scratched at his chin. "Did one of you boys try the taps for some reason?" Neither claimed to have done so.

"Oh man, if it is the pipes, that is the most messed-up plumbing we've ever dealt with then." Aaron groaned. Alex ventured to the hall. He saw a bathroom across the way. His flashlight showed the faded wallpaper and tarnished fixtures. Slowly he turned a tap. Nothing happened. He tried the toilet, adjusting the valve to let water back into the cistern. Again nothing happened. Movement in the corner of his eye. He spun on the spot. Light from the small flashlight flashed out into the empty hall. He swore someone had been there.

Turning back to the dry facilities "Yo, Pops. I don't think it was the..." As he turned back toward the hall, Alex's voice dried up in his throat. A young woman was standing there watching him. "Wow, you startled me..." He wheezed. With widening eyes he realized she was there, but he could still see the wall behind her. Pearly tears ran down her face. Arthur noisily entered the hall, distracting Alex. "Da-Da-Dad..." Alex pointed, his mouth still trying to form words. He looked back at the hall, but the girl was gone.

"What did you say, Alex?" Aaron asked from behind his father.

"Did you see her?" Alex whispered.

"What?" Aaron demanded, cupping a hand to his ear.

"Did you see her?" Alex shouted.

"No." His father replied with a force and determination that was too fast for Alex to believe. An awkward silence stretched as they two men studied each other. Finally, Arthur broke the stalemate. "There is nothing in this house that shouldn't be except for old wiring and plumbing." Arthur's voice betrayed his nerves. "So let's get back to the front room and devise a plan."

"But what?" Aaron started. He paused to gather his thoughts intrigued by his brother's actions. Alex was flashing his light up and down the hall hoping to catch another glimpse of the girl. Aaron seemed to have come to a conclusion. "What the hell was that? The noises I mean, and what is Alex talking about?" he demanded. He turned to his brother, who now stood wide-eyed staring back at him. They looked to their father, who shrugged.

"Old plumbing?" Arthur offered lamely, yet he also glanced around the hall nervously.

"What about the moaning and shit?" Aaron demanded. His father simply shrugged again. Alex shivered, his breath visible in the air. Aaron rubbed at his arms against the chill. "And why the hell is it suddenly so frickin' cold?" The two quickly followed their father back to the warmth of the front room.

PAINFUL NEWS

Hidden in the shadows of the hall, the tears trailed down the young woman's face. "I knew they had to be, but gone? For years?" Her voice was a whisper. "When did Dad die?" She was staring at the faded wallpaper but not seeing it. "Where did they move to?" She pulled her gray-wool coat tighter against the sudden chill in the air. Chloe was unseen by the men. She had heard people enter the house and gone to investigate. Over the years many had entered. Mostly kids on dares; only a few had tried to make the old house a home. None had stayed. She had many times tried to warn all of them, most times just her appearance was enough to send them screaming. This was the first time any had mentioned her. Even the so-called paranormal experts got it wrong. A half-choked laugh sob croaked out as she remembered the "investigation."

"We're trying to contact the spirit who dwells in this space," Linda Blackstone, a famed psychic called. Chloe was sitting in the conservatory lamenting the condition of the once-lush gardens when she heard the call. Chloe had been called many things over the years, the gray ghost, the gray girl, the gray lady, but spirit was new, and if she was honest, a bit insulting. What she didn't know was she was about to become truly annoyed.

Mike Krewleski panned his camera around the cluttered, poorly lit room. Starting wide, he pushed in, getting his subject in the middle of his viewfinder. Meanwhile, Linda held up her hands and wandered through the mess with her eyes half-closed. Mike felt Linda's only power was her ability to navigate in areas like this with her eyes closed. Cutting off the laugh that threatened to escape, he remembered the paycheck and returned to the job at hand. Linda stopped, raised her arms, and dropped her voice to a whisper. "She's here." Linda turned on the spot with her arms out wide as if trying to touch the spirit. Mike couldn't help but roll his eyes. How many times had he followed her into one of these houses? She paused, turned slightly, and addressed the corner of the room. "Spirit, will you communicate with us?" Linda asked in her most mysterious voice. Mike turned a laugh into a cough. It would be the same. Linda would convince herself she felt something or heard something and end up scaring herself in the dark. If it didn't pay so well, he would have told her to drop the farce.

While Mike struggled with trying not to tell Linda she was a fraud, Chloe watched from across the room. She wondered who the woman was talking to as Linda had her back to Chloe and was staring into a corner that was completely empty. Quizzically she watched as Mike moved in close behind Linda.

"Did you feel that?" Linda whispered. Mike was looking around as if he were searching. "Something brushed my arm. I think she is trying to communicate." Linda's voice was hushed.

"There!" Mike pointed to an old lamp. It was a hideous relic with fringe along the bottom of the shade. "Did you see that? It moved!" Mike was now pointing his camera at the motionless lamp. He spun on the spot. "I felt someone touch me," he cried. He smirked behind his lens. He would never win an Academy Award, but it made Linda feel better when he played along.

"Yes, like a hand on my arm. She is trying to tell us she's here." Linda was ecstatic. Chloe laughed. It had been years since she had done so. The effect it had was immediate and hilarious. Mike and Linda spun at the sound. Both eyes wide and terrified, Linda clutched painfully onto Mike's arm. His camera shook. The looks on their faces mixed with the fact that they were still looking in the wrong direction caused Chloe to burst out with laughter again.

Linda forced her voice into its calmest and most ethereal tone. She was addressing a spot several feet to Chloe's right. Her next words ended Chloe's mirth. "Am I speaking to Edgar's young lover who died in this house?"

They couldn't possibly mean me? Chloe thought.

"Are you the spirit of the young girl who went missing?" Linda asked breathlessly. "The one who walks these halls mourning the loss of her true love?" Linda waited for a moment. "Are you the spirit of the girl who loved Edgar Davis but was rejected by his mother and not allowed to marry?" Linda advanced slightly. "Did you kill yourself in this house?"

Chloe glided back, stunned. She was half in the doorway and the wall. She couldn't believe what she was hearing. *Was this what her parents had thought? How could her friends think that after what she had told them?* Chloe's mind was a tumbling mess of questions and horror. *This wasn't happening.* "No!" she cried, immediately covering her mouth. A tense moment passed. Chloe prayed she had not been heard. Just as she began to relax, a rumbling from above sent dust and plaster showering down.

Linda and Mike stood stock still looking up at the ceiling as if to see through it. Linda screwed up her courage. As she opened her mouth to ask another question. "Shush." Chloe immediately hushed her. Chloe could feel the twisting fear in her stomach as its presence grew. A sense, a feeling of anger, guilt, hatred, and pain seeped through the walls surrounding then as it drew ever closer. Chloe fought the urge to run. She didn't like these people and their accusations, but they didn't deserve what was coming.

Linda gasped while Mike's camera crashed to the floor. Chloe appeared before them. "It's coming. You must leave now!" She pointed to the door. Looking past them to the hall, Chloe knew it was almost too late. "Go *now!*" she called.

"Wait, wait, oh my god, a real ghost," Linda stammered. "Was it a broken...?" Her question disappeared as did Chloe. She had warned them. She hoped it was enough. No matter what, Chloe knew better than to stick around when it came. She knew where she was safe, and that is where she was going to be. She cursed her cowardice. She just couldn't be so close to such hatred. She was terrified of him.

Cold tendrils crept down the stairs into the room containing the astonished pair. Linda felt it first, her breath hanging in a cloud in the air. Mike felt it creep up his spine. Foreboding silence enveloped them. The dark corners became black pits as shadows elongated. Linda pressed against Mike, shaking with cold and fear. A black figure slouched into the doorframe. Darkness dripped from it like a liquid. Red coals burned where the eyes should be. A black deeper than any either had witnessed before opened like a mouth below those burning eyes. The howling wind and hate whipped Mike's and Linda's hair and clothes, pushing them to the door. With each step the darkness took, a resounding thud of weight forced down with anger and sadness sounded on the old hardwood floor. The sound sped Linda's and Mike's flight to the door. Mike's already broken camera exploded against the wall inches from his head. Linda fought with the door, trying to prize it open against the tornado-force gusts. The hideous lamp with its fringed shade struck her painfully in the back. A low evil voice was carried on the gale. "Get out." It was barely there but clearly heard. Linda had the door free and was already off the porch before Mike was able to dive through the opening. The door slammed shut, and all was silent again.

Chloe listened to the chaos as she sat safely in the conservatory. She hoped the pair had escaped. The memory faded revealing a surprise to Chloe. Without realizing it she was back in the safety of her conservatory again. She needed to feel safe after listening to Arthur's tale. Instinct at the feeling of cold had sent her there. Her investigating of the new arrivals caused her a pain deep in her core. She did not want to be around when the evil chased them from the house. The face of the young man swam into her mind's eye. The smile that formed was quickly shaken as were certain thoughts she had not had in decades. She remembered the brief tale she had heard. Memories of the words crashed over her. The death of her father tore through her worse than she could have imagined.

Had the rumors of her running off been too much? Had they killed him? Did he believe the story about her and Edgar? He had had a weak heart since being wounded in the Great War. Could the stress of it all have been too much? Chloe felt the tears falling. She was lost in questions. What happened to her mother and brother after he died? Why didn't he come to find her? Why didn't he help her leave this hell and house? All these questions fought for dominance, causing her head to spin. She let loose a cry of sorrow that echoed through the house. Her legs seemed to give out as she leaned against a pedestal that held a bust of Venus. The weight of her sorrow made her solid enough to send the sculpture crashing to the ground. It wasn't often she could interact with the world around her, so the surprise of it brought her back to reality. There were people in the house. The sound would definitely draw them to her room. They knew some of her story. A drop of hope in the empty space where her heart once beat. Maybe they could help set her story straight. Maybe they could help her finally leave this place. She looked up at the ceiling. "If they don't get run off by the creature upstairs." She sighed.

MAYBE TOMORROW

On the landing of the second floor crouched the shadow of pure anger and hatred. Cold tendrils cascaded down the stairs like fog spreading from the lake. It filled the hall the men had just vacated. She had been there to torment him again. She was always there. A crashing in the conservatory told him she was gone. It was the one place he would never go. Heavy footfalls retreated to the lonely room at the end of the hall. Before the door shut the shadow let loose one last howl of anger and despair. On the other side of the wall a scratching mixed with soft evil laughing.

"Um. So...there's that," Alex whispered, pointing to the crashing sound and the moaning. Standing there with his arms crossed, pointing in different directions, he started to feel better. The chill and sadness seemed to slowly lift from the house. It was quiet again. "So, Dad..." Alex swallowed. "You were saying about Granddad finding something." He glanced up at the ceiling as his arms fell to his sides. "Something that might explain why this house is...groaning?"

Visibly shaken yet trying to hide it with work, Arthur shook his head. Suddenly he looked up at his sons. He jumped as if just realizing they were there. "What? Oh, right." Wiping the sweat from his brow and scratching his chin, he continued the story. "He said he was walking along the old road." Arthur's eyes darted around trying to see into the shadows. "He and his friend were messing around, tossing a football or something." He quickly threw light into an empty corner. Slowly he began to continue. "Well, it bounced over into a field." He adjusted the light, trying to get a better illumination in the space, though he seemed lost in thought. He tried to swallow though his throat was a desert. "Not bad once we get the junk out of here." He started clearing away dust and debris. He could feel the eyes on him. He stopped and turned to his boys. The looks on their faces told him little work was going to get done. Frowning at them, he waited, and then it hit him. "Oh, yeah, the story." He replied to the frowns he was getting. "Well, he went into the field and found..." He watched their faces, "a shoe." He ended, waving his fingers mysteriously, although his eyes nervously scanning every direction ruined the effect.

"A friggin' shoe? How the hell does that mean old Eddy killed her?" Aaron demanded. Alex thought this was obvious.

"Because when he hit her, her shoe flew off. It was proof she didn't just skip town," Alex stated as if saying one and one make two.

"How did he know it was hers and not just a random shoe?" Aaron retorted. There was creaking brought on by a strong wind. Aaron spun in fright then immediately laughed it off. "Jumping at shadows." He muttered to himself. "There might be structural issues. That is where all the noise is coming from," he said bravely.

Arnold nodded, but he wasn't listening. "Well, Granddad was pretty sure about it. Says it was just like the ones she wore." Arnold shrugged. His voice was calm, yet Alex saw his father's eyes glancing to the hall every few seconds. Alex could feel his tension. There was more that wasn't being told.

"Old Granddad had a shoe fetish, huh? Just like Alex." Aaron barked out a laugh. Alex threw a punch at his brother's shoulder, ending up in a headlock for his trouble.

"Boys! This place ain't going to fix itself. Let's get some work done."

"OK, OK! Geoff me." Alex tried to pretend he hadn't seen what he thought he saw and that all he had heard was old plumbing or the wind or whatever people blamed a vision of a ghostly girl on. Checking over his shoulder again, he decided to investigate things a bit more.

"Hey, what about the rumor she was going to marry that Eddy guy?" Aaron suddenly asked, standing up straight. "I just remembered something about that from school. Kids would dare each other to come out here because of the gray girl." He ended sheepishly, remembering his own adventure to the house.

"Shouldn't she be in white?" Alex asked even though he knew the girl he had seen was in gray.

"Like I told you boys, Granddad knew her. She had been complaining about Edgar the morning she went missing." Arthur paused, trying to remember the details. "It seems he tried to pick her up that day." A smile crept into the corners of his mouth. "I guess she had a boyfriend or something at the school that she told him about. Not sure, Dad was always kinda squirrelly about that." Arnold laughed. "You know what?" He watched as his sons stood waiting for the next part of the story. "It's late, and we are not getting anything done." He ignored their groans. "Let's start again tomorrow after you boys get over the ghost stories and scary noises." He laughed. "Tomorrow will be a bright, sunny day, and you'll be ready to work."

1932

The panic started at his toes and quickly filled Edgar like a beer poured too quickly in a glass. It spilled over into jittery terror clouding his vision twice as bad as the booze. "This wasn't what you thought this night was going to be like," he heard through the haze.

"What do I do? What do I do?" he whimpered. "Oh god, if she had been dead..." Not sure how that would be better, Edgar felt his train of thought derail.

Then it was there again, that voice softly in his ear: "Come on; she's not long for this world."

Edgar nodded in agreement. "That's true, but what if they find her body? Maybe I should go get help," Edgar whispered. He moved toward the cab; the bottle in his hand clanked against the fender. He looked at it. He could see the liquid swirling in the almost empty vessel.

"No, they can never find the body," he heard a voice say. He knew what he had to do now. Quickly finishing the bottle, he tossed the empty into the bed of the truck. Expecting to hear it shatter or clatter, Edgar was confused for a second by the dull thud. His eyes grew accustomed to the dark while a sigh of relief escaped his lips. Looking in the bed of the truck, he could make out the outline of the tarp covering the boxes of dynamite he had picked up. His father wanted him to demolish an old well on the property in preparation for an expansion on the house. "Yeah, just wrap her up in that."

Chloe's agonized screams pierced Edgar's ears as he pulled her broken body to the tailgate. Trying to find a way to lift her without causing more screams, he paused to pull an old rag from his pocket. Wiping his brow he held onto the filthy cloth for a moment; the next moment he found it stuffed into her mouth. It muffled the cries as he lifted her into the bed and covered her in the tarp. He ignored her muffled whimpering as he turned to search for anything left behind. The drink still clouded his vision; his shaking hands gathered up anything he could find. Her books flew into the bed, causing a cry out through the cloth. He was in the cab wiping the sweat from his brow with the shaking back of his hand. The drive was now a blur. He could hear her crying with every bump. The truck slowed to a crawl. Rolling down the long drive to the estate, he checked his watch. It was only six fifteen. Perfect, their father never left the office before six thirty. His mother would already be several glasses of gin gone. He would not be noticed.

The truck eased around the house to where timbers were already in place for the expansion. The truck backed slowly to the edge; he began to calm down. Edgar found himself next to the old well. It was all going to be over in a few minutes. Dump the body and the explosives, come back tomorrow and blow the well. It would cave in on itself. The workers would fill it in the rest of the way then build the extension. She'd never be found under the concrete.

His calm was tested when he pulled the tarp off. Chloe's eyes were wide, her face stained with tears. There was blood on the corners of her mouth. Edgar stumbled back as she tried to pull the gag out. The hand pawed at her face; the arm was too broken or weak to do the job. Terrified, he pulled her by the shattered legs. They felt all wrong in his hands. He reached up to her hips to get a better hold. The feeling reminded him of bags of gravel he used to carry. He knew the bones were destroyed. Tears were rolling down his cheeks. He tried to hum a tune to drown out the muffled cries. Avoiding her pleading eyes, he grabbed her around the chest. It, too, gave under the pressure; he was sure many of the ribs were broken. She wouldn't last long, especially after the fall. Dragging her off the tailgate, he pushed her battered body into the well. She fell like a sack of potatoes into the darkness. Edgar leaned over the edge breathing heavily, fighting back the urge to be sick. He listened for any sound. All he heard was the usual noise of the night. After several minutes, he was sure she was dead. He found another bottle of whiskey in his shaking hands. It burned his throat as he drank deeply. "It's all going to be fine."

RING OF LIGHT

Through the blinding pain, Chloe was aware she was cold and wet. She also began to figure out that her foot was lying on her upper arm. She tried to call out, but each breath felt like a knife being plunged into her chest. She already knew she would never walk again. This thought brought her pain, not for herself but for Rupert Holt, her friend. He had finally started to move things forward by asking her to the winter dance. He would be so disappointed. She thought of her mother and how she could never help her with the housework and the baking. She cried for her brother, who she would never get to play with again. He would grow up with an invalid as a sister. Her poor father—she would no longer be able to assist him in his machinery shop. She so loved fixing the old tractors and cars the farmers brought in. Her small hands had been so helpful in the tight spaces. Her mother had been so proud when Chloe was accepted into college, the first in the family—especially since Chloe was a woman. She was only eighteen; she'd have a long life to be in a wheelchair. So her thoughts went.

As the night wore on and the cold crept deep, she began to understand and accept that she wasn't going to be in a wheelchair; she was never leaving this hole. Morning found her weak; her breathing was shallow. Each breath was agony. She could see the morning sunlight far above. It was a beautiful blue-sky morning. Chloe wished she could feel its warmth. She could feel very little now. Darkness was closing in, but it was not relief. It was a shadow blocking out the view. Wood scraping on stone, a thud as a heavy box crashed down beside her. Then another, then a third that severed what was left of her right arm. She saw the stump but felt no pain; it barely bled. A sizzle from far off came closer and closer until a stick and fuse lay burning on her once-beautiful gray-wool coat. The bright flash ended her pain.

Edgar smiled in relief, dabbing at the sweat on his brow. While the smoke still billowed out of the well, he fought to keep himself upright. The adrenaline and relief mixed with the hangover fought to take his consciousness. He could taste the bile in the back of his throat. The edges of the well tumbled in. Edgar called for some workmen to come fill the rest of the hole. Edgar's brother Richard stood on the back porch watching the work. Edgar felt his stomach turn over as he watched Richard eat a plate of eggs. "'Bout time you got this done," Richard called. Edgar replied with just a short wave.

"Damn! There must have been an animal down there when it blew," a burly workman called out, holding a bloody mess on the end of a shovel.

Edgar's already-pale skin reached a new level of white. "Oh, that is gruesome." Richard laughed. "What do you think, Edgar?" He patted Edgar on the shoulder as Edgar's hands hit his knees. If his stomach hadn't been empty, its contents would be on the ground at his feet. As it was all he could do was dry heave his bile. "Just chuck it in the hole and cover it, will you?" Richard smirked as he turned back toward the house, leaving Edgar to fight through his sickness.

When Edgar went in to town later to get the truck fixed, the story of the deer being hit was completely accepted. The panic and sickness returned when news of the local girl going missing hit the papers. He fought it in his usual manner, by blotting it out with drink. When the police came to question Edgar after reports that he had spoken to the missing girl on the morning of the day she went missing, Edgar's father initially refused to let them even speak to him. Richard even said that he stopped in to see Edgar after he left the office, and Edgar was still busy at the mill. When Edgar finally was allowed to speak, he explained he had offered the young woman a ride on that cold morning, as any man of good breeding would. She went missing right after school, and since Edgar was in his office working on paperwork at that time, he couldn't have had anything to do with it. The police apologized for bothering such a well-respected and connected family. After that the investigation turned into just another runaway eighteen-year-old girl looking for a life in the big city. This never sat well with Chloe's family and friends. Edgar would often ignore the dirty looks he received in town. He got used to the young man following him, watching where he went. After a couple of years, Edgar would take pleasure in knowing Chloe's body was beneath the floor of their conservatory. After these thoughts he would drink until he couldn't feel the guilt or anything else anymore.

WHAT AN ODDITY

Slowly thoughts began to creep back into Chloe's mind. She became aware of the blackness surrounding her. The closeness of the space pressed in on her. It was then she realized she could feel it in her arms. She could feel it in her legs. Everything was back in its correct position. She felt complete but not whole. There was a pounding far, far above her. She pulled a hand to her chest. It was difficult, heavy, like moving through thick, muddy water. When her fingers brushed the wool of the jacket, the coarse material under her finger brought back something; she felt comfort. Her father had bought it for her. It was special, warm, and felt like home. It was his gift to keep her warm at college. She pulled her other arm in to her neck. Her fingers searched but could not find the fine, thin gold chain or the cross that was a gift from her mother. Chloe curled and uncurled her toes. It was odd. She could tell she was wearing only one shoe. Her movements felt like she was swimming underwater, but she could breathe. Then she thought for a moment, could she? She focused on her lungs, trying to tell if she could or did breathe. Her body gave no evidence of whether it needed oxygen or not.

Chloe became aware that the pounding had stopped at some point. Time didn't seem to matter here. She didn't know if it was day or night. As she existed in the darkness, she might have been there an hour or a day. She felt no weight. She was simply there, never hungry, never tired; nothing hurt. It was just dark and lonely. She tried to move and found she could. It was difficult but not impossible *If it feels like swimming then perhaps it is like swimming,* Chloe thought for a moment. It was odd she wasn't completely sure which way was up. Making the decision she began to *swim*. She never felt tired, but after not being able to tell how long it had been, she became discouraged.

Chloe began to lose faith. Anger flash into her mind as she felt she wasn't getting any nearer her goal. Then depression would creep in, causing her to stop several times. She would exist for a while just being in the darkness. Then the panic would overtake her. She wanted to see; she wanted to be free. It had gone on too long. She was tired, not physically, just tired of the dark, tired of being alone. She was done with the dark; frustrated and defeated, she wanted to scream, to cry out. Not sure what would happen and not really caring, she remembered how it felt to fill her lungs, how to make the sound. She was about to scream when suddenly, *Voices!* She heard voices, low at first but increasing in volume. Chloe *swam* toward them. Clearer and clearer they became. She was catching bits of conversation.

"I was sent here to fix the problems," a man's voice explained. There was something in this voice that made her slow down. It was not the type of voice she would have been comfortable to be around. There was another voice now, a common rough type. This was the type she would always avoid. She knew it well from men who would come into her father's shop. They would say things that made her uncomfortable, and the looks they would give her made her skin crawl. She felt whoever was on the receiving end of this line of questioning was not in a good position.

"Father left Richard everything of any worth," was the reply. This voice was more refined, but it held a tone of contempt Chloe recognized as Edgar's voice. She froze in her advance. There was some indiscernible arguing, followed by a distant bang, then nothing. Silence followed for some time. Chloe did not move for a long period. Again time seemed to have no hold here, but Chloe tried to judge as best she could. Finally she felt it safe to start moving again. When next she heard voices they were very clear and not the same ones she had heard before.

"This addition was finished in 1933, creating the conservatory." Another voice Chloe did not recognize, but she used it as a beacon to follow. She moved in the direction. It felt like forever; the frustration started to build again. Finally she hit a barrier. It was something that resisted her movement. She could feel it. It was rough and solid. She had come so far, or she felt she had. Now she was stuck. Angry, Chloe pushed harder on the barrier.

"No, no, no!" she cried, small fists pounding at the blockade. Suddenly she felt it give way. She was free of the dark and the pressure. Her hands grasped at nothing then felt the hard concrete. She pulled her head free and then her body was out. She was standing in a room with a glass ceiling and walls. She was surrounded by various plants and several pieces of comfortable furniture. Other than a few stone busts that stared at her with sightless eyes, she was alone. Listening for the voices Chloe heard nothing. She raised her hands to her mouth to call out. It took just a moment to realize what she was seeing. When she understood it, she was screaming. Chloe could see through her hands. They were there, she could feel them, but they were transparent. She was staring at her hands, panic again in her brain. She couldn't believe what she was seeing, what she knew she was. Suddenly Chloe looked up at the sound of feet running toward her.

1936

Edgar lay slumped against an old fallen tree. He was wet and cold. His head was pounding, and what little contents were in his stomach threatened to rebel. That would be the last time he bought moonshine from old Jake. The sun was barely beginning to show above the mountains when Edgar's vision cleared enough to see the hand barely visible under a pile of leaves. Slowly he crept forward, startled by the clatter of his hunting rifle falling from his lap. He leaped back, holding his breath. The hand didn't move.

"No, no, no," he muttered, moving again closer to the mound of leaves. The musky dampness mingled with a sweat perfume. Brushing away the leaves and dirt revealed a young woman's face. Her eyes were open, and her face still held the look of shock. Brushing more detritus off of the corpse, Edgar could see the large, damp red stain in her disheveled clothes. It was then he noticed the red covering his hands.

Edgar scuttled back to the fallen log, quickly checking his rifle. He was missing a bullet. He found the casing nearby. "I must have shot her when I was drunk." He whimpered. "Not again, not again. I can't go through this again."

There it was again, that soft whisper in his ear. "That's OK; these things happen." Edgar stared at the dead girl. She looked familiar. "What you have to ask is why was she out in the woods at night?" Edgar studied the face. Finally it hit him. She was a waitress at a diner in town. He had asked her out once or twice, even offering her a ride home a couple of other times. Every time she had refused him.

"She lives on the other side of town," Edgar slurred. "Why is she out here?" He got unsteadily to his feet. Stumbling in a circle, he tried to figure out where she had come from. He was about twenty feet into the woods. The spot lay just in view of a small pasture on the back property of his house. He could see one of the chimneys just above the trees on the other side of the clearing.

"This is private property." Edgar nodded. "No one comes back here." Edgar was looking around trying to see if anyone else was around. "Just cover the body back up and leave it to nature to take care of. She'll never be missed. Just like all the other girls who have run off to the city to find better fortunes." Edgar laughed, immediately covering his mouth as the implication of his statement threatened to infect his mind. Through the stupor he covered the body with more dirt and leaves. Bending over to cover the girl's face, the drink kicked back in, causing him to fall. The girl groaned as Edgar's weight pushed air out of her lungs. He was back against the log, pointing at the corpse with a shaking finger. "No, no, it's all right. She's dead. Just cover her up, and we can go home." Edgar closed his eyes tightly, praying when he opened them again that he would be back in his bed. He counted to ten and opened his eyes. She was still there. He knew what he had to do. Pushing himself up, he found a bottle next to his feet. Taking a long drink to steady his nerves, Edgar continued to cover the body.

The sun was fully up and shone bright when he returned to the house. Richard was there to help him up the porch steps. Edgar swayed dangerously. "You were out all night. Then you come home drunk and filthy," Richard chastised. "Mother will not be pleased. To say nothing of what father will think." Richard pulled his brother through the empty sitting room. "Best to just get you to bed. I'll tell them you've taken ill," he explained pulling Edgar up the stairs.

"Thank you, Richard," Edgar slurred. "You are always looking out for me."

"Yes, and I always will, dear brother of mine."

Unwelcome Guests

A rush of running feet ended as a woman clattered into the room. With a squeak she skidded to a halt at the sight of Chloe. Another woman and man followed close on her heels. They rushed in, skidding to a halt behind the first woman. The new arrivals stared for a second, then the new woman began to scream. She was pointing at Chloe. Chloe screamed back in terror staring through a hand at the couple. The woman was bustled out of the conservatory by the man while the first woman stood rooted to the spot. Chloe reached out to her for help.

The woman's scream drowned out Chloe's cries. In a flash the woman disappeared through the door. Chloe followed pleading. "Please help me! I don't understand." In an instant Chloe halted. She realized she was gliding after the woman. It was fortunate that she did, as the woman had come to a complete stop. At the foot of a grand staircase, huddled together on the floor, were the man and woman who had fled earlier. The other woman's head spun between Chloe and the couple. Darkness and cold seeped down the stairs like a fog rolling in. The heavy sounds of footfalls echoed from above them. Chloe could feel the anger, the hatred, and the despair creeping closer.

The man had struggled to his feet now. He half-carried, half-dragged the woman away. Chloe heard the front door slam but found herself still staring up the stairs waiting for the horror to appear. The woman who had arrived last whispered, "Who's there?" as she tried to back away and put distance between herself and the unseen. Her attention was completely held by the dark at the top of the stairs. She ignored Chloe floating just behind her.

The woman's voice increased in volume. "This is not funny! I demand to know who is here." She waited for a reply. When none came she continued. "I am a representative of the estate and demand that you vaca—" An angry wind blew down the stairs, knocking the woman into a chair.

Darkness descended the stairs, flowing and collapsing in on itself and reforming. Chloe's back was against the wall. The woman pushed herself to her feet. Before their horrified eyes, the darkness materialized into a beast. Its gaze held them with glowing embers for eyes and shadows melting off and reforming over it. Advancing on the woman, the creature radiated hate.

"Get out," the beast rasped. In an instant the woman abandoned her backward retreating in favor of a full pelt to the door.

She was alone now with the creature. Chloe tried to melt away before being noticed. Her movement caught the darkness's attention. The eyes turned to flames; the fires of hell erupted in the thing's mouth. Through the howl of rage, a chorus of demons shouted *"Youuuuu!"* Tendrils of black shot from the pointing finger toward Chloe. She screamed, then was silenced as she found herself in another room. She had slid through a wall.

Getting her bearings, she flew back to the conservatory. Shaking with terror, she hid in a flowerbed. Listening for any sound, she lay still and quiet. Nothing was pursuing her. She stayed there for hours trying to make sense of what had happened. After a while, when she was sure the thing she had seen was not going to come for her, emerging from the dirt, she began to explore the massive house, her feet barely making contact with the floor. It was an odd feeling. The more she moved, the more she enjoyed it. She floated from room to room on the main floor. All of the furniture was covered in dusty cloths, and the house was still. It felt abandoned. Listening to the silence, she got the feeling that no one had been living here for a long time. When she had finished her exploration, she found herself at the bottom of the stairs again. It was quiet. The air held none of the malevolence it had earlier. Tentatively, she began to ascend.

At the top of the stairs, a long, wide hall contained many portraits of stern-looking men. The last in the line was a face she recognized. A tear ran down her transparent face. Chloe knew where she was now. She was in Sterben Hall. Fear gripped her. "Edgar," She breathed. Willing her body to move faster, her feet kicking frantically at the air, finally through determination she flew down the stairs to the front door. Her hand went through again, and again she tried. Her fingers could not grasp the handle. She was trapped! She had to flee. Chloe was flying back down the hall. She was back in the conservatory and back in the dirt. It took several long, panicked moments to calm her mind enough to come to some conclusions, the first of which was she was alone. No one followed, and she heard no sound. There was something in the house, but it didn't seem to know she was there. She thought back to the picture and to Edgar. She had risen from her hiding place without realizing it. She was floating around looking at the dried flowers and blank stares of the busts. She was in front of a statue of a woman holding a vase.

"That really isn't dignified, you know?" she asked the statue. "You'd think you'd notice your breast hanging out like that." She received no answer. "You know, I think my fears of Edgar finding and hurting me are a bit unfounded." She was now talking to a bust of Caesar. "I think I get it now." She held up her hand. Looking through it, she continued. "I'm already dead, so what can he do to me?" She was wandering back up the hall. Stopping in front of a painting of a boy fishing, she sniffed at the dust. "By the look of some of the things in the house, I think I have been for a while." She was back at the front door. Again her hand slipped straight through. She addressed the door. "Not being able to use the door knob is no big deal." She shrugged. "After all, I passed through the floor and a wall." Chloe pushed herself against the wooden door. It resisted at first, then she was outside the house. Late afternoon sunlight streamed onto the wide front porch.

Looking down, she could barely be seen in the sunlight. This would be a small problem when she got home. She had to see her parents, tell them what had happened, and make sure Edgar never took someone else's daughter from them. Mind made up, she marched down the steps to the path. She could feel a tug at her back with every step she took. Pain began to creep up her arms, her legs, and her chest. It was difficult to walk. The tug became a pull. Chloe felt every broken bone, every injury from being hit then dumped down the well. The pain was too intense; she gave up the struggle. She watched as she was pulled back up the walk. The lane grew farther and farther away; the pain receded. She was back on the porch, through the door, down the hall but stopped in the conservatory. She was complete free from physical pain again, but the tears returned often.

The conservatory is where she spent most of her time. As time wore on, she found she could interact with objects. This was a blessing to her, for she could read all the books in the massive library. Only once more did she venture upstairs. She reached what she could only assume was the master bedroom. She could feel hatred seeping out under the door and knew she did not want to enter there. Then there was the scratching and the breathing that seemed to follow her through the halls when she ventured close to the stairs. So she *haunted* the library and conservatory. This thought always brought a wry smile to her face.

WHAT GRANDDAD KNEW

The face of the girl was there every time Alex closed his eyes. She had a very pretty face, but she was sad. Then there were her eyes. They held so much surprise and wonder yet so much pain. Alex so wanted to see her again. There was something about her. Something he needed to know. He felt he needed to help her, protect her. Shaking the thought from his head, he grumbled to himself, "Chauvinist much?" He had tried to get his father to tell more of the story on the drive home, but the older man wouldn't give up any additional information.

"Granddad had some strange ideas. He was obsessed with that girl and that house" was all Alex could get from him. The conversation ended as they pulled into the drive. Once in the house, Alex tried to bring it up again. At this point Arthur told Alex. "If you want to know"—he pointed down the hall— "you're more than welcome to go through his stuff." Alex stared down the semidark passage to the closed door at the end. This had been his grandfather's room. Since his death the room had become more and more of a storeroom. Alex nodded, unsure of how he wanted to proceed. He had fond memories of his granddad. He had come to live with them after Alex's grandmother had died in the same car accident that had taken Alex's mother. His granddad's room was not somewhere he ventured often. A few times he remembered sitting at the desk in the corner while his granddad told him stories about World War II or the town's history. Most times it felt as if he was intruding on a very special sanctuary when the old man lived there and more so since his death.

"Granddad was obsessed with her?" Alex found it odd that the girl in the gray coat was never mentioned by the older man. Alex found his hand on the door handle. Taking a deep breath, he turned the knob. Darkness stared back at him. The familiar smell of Old Spice and cigars sent memories chasing through Alex's mind. Focusing on the task at hand, he flicked the light on. The atmosphere was immediately broken by the disarray of the room. Several boxes lay scattered where his grandfather's bed had been. Since his granddad's passing, that was the only piece of furniture that had been removed. Alex knew his father kept putting off cleaning out the room. Aaron was responsible for the scattered boxes. Even he seemed to feel he was intruding. Other than the missing bed and boxes, the room looked like it always had. One painting of a field on the wall, some old photos on the desk, but mostly it was very Spartan. Alex had never really paid attention to the photos before. He always assumed it was just pictures of the family. He sat wearily on the old, hard chair and began to really look at the faces in the old frames. Pictures of his father when he was young, his granddad and grandma in front of a house, and the usual things he expected. What he didn't expect to see was Sterben Hall. Standing in front of the huge manor was a rather severe-looking couple with several children. The woman in the picture resembled his grandmother.

Alex began to go through the desk drawers. He found Christmas cards he and his brother had made when they were kids, old bank statements, and random documents that held no meaning or importance now. Next he grabbed one of the boxes labeled *Pictures* from the floor. He felt almost like an archaeologist as he began to delve deeper into the box. Polaroids gave way to smaller reddened photos, then to black-and-white pictures of Granddad in his army uniform. Near the bottom he found pictures of children he did not recognize. It was on one of those large, long panoramic-type pictures of children that his eyes deceived him. He swore it moved toward his hand. He rubbed his eyes and watched the rolled up paper. Nothing happened. After an uncomfortable shrug, he unrolled the picture. Written on one corner was *Lafayette High School 1932*. Alex picked up a magnifying glass from the desk and began to study the faces. It took a few moments of scrutinizing before he found his granddad. With a gasp, Alex drew the picture and glass closer to his eye. Standing next to his grandfather, with a beautiful happy smile, was the girl he had seen at Sterben Hall. "Granddad did know her," he whispered.

Box tops lay strewn around the room; papers lay piled one on top of the other ankle deep. It was getting near midnight when Alex found the artifact that lay open in his lap. It was a journal kept by his granddad about Chloe Miller, who had gone missing in their senior year. In the same box as the journal was a girl's black-and-white leather shoe. It had a short heel and laces. Alex couldn't believe it had been kept all this time.

Opening the journal carefully—the yellowing pages were brittle—Alex noticed the journal began before the disappearance.

September 26, 1932

It is the first day of school. The summer was rough, still not a lot of work to be had. What few jobs were available at the mill went fast at the end of last year. Mother didn't want me working, but I know we could have used the extra money. I saw Chloe today. She was a pretty as ever. This might be the year I finally ask her out.

Alex flipped through several entries that spoke mostly of school, the few opportunities in town, and how his father had finally found a job at the mill after an accident had killed the previous employee. It wasn't until October that Chloe was mentioned again.

October 21, 1932

I was walking with Chloe after school today when she asked if I was going to go to the Halloween parade next Saturday. When I said I was considering it, she told me she was going, and we should meet up. I think she might fancy me as I do her. I agreed, so I will have to see how it goes. It is going to be a long wait until next Saturday.

October 30, 1932

Yesterday was fantastic. Chloe and I spent time watching the parade and talking. We stopped in at the drugstore and had a soda. She was so pretty. I lay my hand on hers while we sat drinking, and it was perfect until that foul Edgar Davis walked in. He kept staring at us. Chloe was sure he was drunk. He comes from a well-respected family in town. His brother is well liked, but Edgar is cruel and always intoxicated. I wish I could find out where he got his liquor and get him arrested. I mentioned this to Chloe, but she told me to be careful since my dad works for Edgar's family. I think this town would be better off without him. I wish his brother ran the mill. It wouldn't be so dangerous there if he did.

November 18, 1932

There was an announcement today. Next month we are going to have a dance. They call it the Snow Ball. I asked Chloe if she wanted to go with me, and she said yes. I can't believe it. She seemed really happy I asked. Tommy Kent was laughing at me when I did it. He didn't laugh when she said yes.

November 30, 1932

Chloe was complaining about that Edgar Davis again. He had tried to pick her up on the way to school today. She was able to get away from that dirty drunk, but she was pretty upset. I wanted to walk her home, but I had to help Mother run some errands. I told her about Edgar, and all she could say was he came from a good family, and we shouldn't look badly at him. He kept a lot of families working at the mill.

December 1, 1932

Chloe wasn't at school today. I felt sick all day with worry. I went to her house after school, but she hadn't come home the night before. They were worried something fierce. I retraced the path back to school and found some papers but no sign of her. I found skid marks and some weird marks on the ground but nothing else. Tomorrow I am going to go to Sterben Hall to see what I can find out.

December 2, 1932

I met Richard Davis today. He was very pleasant if not a bit aloof. I asked after Edgar and where he was yesterday. Richard mentioned Edgar offering Chloe a ride. He told me she had told Edgar she was thinking of leaving town to find work in the city. I did not believe him—Edgar that is. Richard then explained he had met his brother at the mill after 7:00 p.m., and they had been together there until after nine. The girl had been reported missing around 6:00 p.m., so Edgar couldn't have had anything to do with it. When I asked about damage I saw to Edgar's truck, Richard said he had hit a deer. I think he is covering for his no-good brother. Tommy says they don't want a scandal.

December 10, 1932

Tommy's family lives near Chloe's family. I walked home with him yesterday. Today I took him to where I found the paper and the weird marks on the side of the road. We spent some time searching around. He found stains in the dirt that looked like blood, and somebody tried to cover it. I mentioned the deer, but Tommy didn't know why Edgar would be out this way. He kicked a stone into the field; I don't know why but I watched it fly; it was then I saw something. I found Chloe's shoe. I know something happened to her.

December 11, 1932

I told the police what I found and about Edgar's truck. They told me they had already talked to Edgar and his family. He had an alibi, but it was obvious Chloe had run off. She wasn't the first, they said. I told them Chloe would never do that. Tommy's uncle is a deputy, and he said I was just upset because I was sweet on her and she'd run off. I told him she would not leave her family; they were too close. They finally got mad and told me to leave.

December 27, 1932

I have been following Edgar whenever I can. I know Chloe must be dead by now. But I keep hoping that maybe Edgar just has her stashed somewhere. My parents are upset because I have missed school a lot lately, and Dad had seen me hanging round the mill.

January 26, 1933

Edgar threatened my dad today. He has seen me snooping around and asking questions. He told my dad that if I keep making trouble, then he would fire him. It isn't fair. No one saw Edgar in his office. No one saw Richard come in. The front of Edgar's truck was messed up. Then I found Chloe's shoe and blood on the road. No one will believe me. I know Edgar killed her.

February 14, 1933

I miss Chloe. I haven't found anything new to prove Edgar Davis killed her, but I know she must be dead. She never contacted her family or me. Edgar knows I know. Every time he sees me, he gets angry.

Alex flipped through the rest of the journal. There were mentions of other girls going missing and how his granddad had done more investigating and talking to the police to no avail. The journaling stopped in 1934 after his granddad left for college. It didn't start again until 1939 when he joined the army. Alex was surprised to see a picture of his granddad standing with other soldiers in front of a B-17 bomber emblazoned with the name Chloe. He hadn't even known his granddad had been a pilot.

Getting to his feet and stretching his aching back, Alex watched a news clipping flutter out of the back of the journal. The clipping was dated 1949. The story told of how Edgar Davis was found dead in Sterben Hall, apparently the victim of a robbery gone wrong. Edgar was shot in his bed. He was survived by his brother, Richard Davis, of Pittsburgh. Alex dismissed the thought that his grandfather may have had a hand in Edgar's death. He turned off the light and closed the door to the room, the picture, clipping, and journal still tucked under his arm. He decided to find out whatever happened to Richard Davis and see if they ever found out who had killed Edgar. On top of that, he had to tell his father and brother that they had bought a murder house.

Still Tied and Bound

"I guess it could be worse." Chloe shrugged to the girl with the vase statue. "I have the run of the place." She looked at the scattered books that littered the conservatory. It was true that she had free run of the downstairs of the grand old house. Rarely did the evil from upstairs venture out of the master bedroom. Even though she had books and the ability to go outside, she could never go more than a few feet from the house before the pain started. Over the years Chloe tried many times to leave the grounds of Sterben Hall. She had made it to the road once. It was after that time that she had given up, resigning to spend her days in the house. Time slipped by. Chloe did not need to sleep, but she found that she would become unaware of the passage of time.

She became used to being alone in the house. Neither the couple nor the woman had ever returned to the house. It was as if she would suddenly notice that time had passed. She watched as the once-proud house became rundown and cold. Children would throw rocks through the windows or sneak in to smoke and drink. This kind of disrespect annoyed her. Chloe had come to think of the empty house as her home. Times when it looked like something untoward was going to happen she would make her presence known. Whether it was blowing out candles or a well-placed groan, it generally had the same effect. She would be left alone again. When her haunting did not have the desired effect, the outcome was still the same. The people would find their way upstairs, and when that happened, it was guaranteed they would never return. The seeping anger chased everyone away.

Chloe was floating over the spot on the floor where the old well was. The late-day sun caused her to be completely transparent. She was having a staring contest with the cold-stone eyes of an ugly bust of a Greek goddess when she became aware of a sweeping sound in the conservatory. Looking over the goddess's head, she noticed several men and an older woman cleaning up the dead plants. Intrigued, she decided to watch for a while. This wasn't the usual intruders. Bright light returned to the conservatory over the next few days as the windows were cleaned. All through the rest of the house, the boards were removed and windows replaced. During the day it was a flurry of activity. Cleaning and moving and banging. Chloe feared they would awaken the thing upstairs. The workmen never seemed too interested in going up to the second floor. They would take some of the old furniture up there but quickly return.

Chloe thought it was odd that several of the pieces of really fine furniture were moved to the front room. Over several weeks the group added many other antiques and oddities. They filled the dining room with dishes and hutches and display cabinets. The conservatory was again full of plants and old gardening equipment. Books were added to the library; they were all older-looking books, but they were new to Chloe. Tables and cabinets covered the halls, the formal living room, and the billiard room, everywhere. Chloe found this very strange. Then one day people began to come to the house. They came and went, buying and selling curious things. Some of her statue friends were carried away, but new ones came in to replace them.

Chloe liked having people in the house. She liked the noise, the smells, and the conversations. She didn't understand some of the things they talked about, but she was interested. She did notice that furniture that was original to the house was never sold. People would get near it then quickly move away. This made Chloe happy. She felt connected to the furnishings and did not want any of it to go. Then one day something happened that altered Chloe's world. Some old magazines began to show up. She recognized *Life* and *Time* and a few others. She saw some that she had actually read before she died. Then she would look through these after all the people left. She found out about the Second World War, Vietnam, civil rights, and, to her astonishment, the moon landing. So much had changed; if she could leave the grounds, would she even recognize the world? With every new acquisition, Chloe would get excited. This meant something new for her to learn about or remember. Then after a couple of years, something happened that changed the house and Chloe's world yet again.

A large truck pulled up to the house. Men began to unload a lot of bedroom furniture. Chloe thought very little of it until the men began to move the ropes that blocked off the stairs. They were taking the furniture up there and making a lot of noise. After the second load was up the stairs, she knew there was trouble.

"I didn't think it was that cold out." The woman shivered heading to close the open front door. Reaching it, she felt warm. "That is odd." Somewhere above her a door slammed. There was a tremendous crash followed by a thundering of feet on the stairs. "My word! Is everyone all right?" the woman shouted.

Wide-eyed with terror, a man skidded to a halt in front of the woman. "Mrs. Sellers! There is something up there. I'm not waiting around to find out what it is," a workman explained. He glanced back up the stairs then hurried for the door. The second man bounded down the stairs and out the door without a word to Mrs. Sellers. Chloe knew they had disturbed it.

"For heaven's sake!" Mrs. Sellers exclaimed, heading to the stairs. Chloe flew to her, making herself known. She appeared on the stair right in front of the very shocked woman. Mrs. Sellers screamed at the appearance of a transparent girl. Her scream felt like it pierced Chloe's head. She knew it was the . scream that sent the sensation through her. There was cold and hate flowing around her. Despair as Chloe had never known filled her. Mrs. Sellers was running for the door now. Chloe was backing away from the darkness. It spread and pooled and flowed like smoke slowly forming a hulking creature with burning eyes. Chloe backed away. A tongue of shadow flicked out at her. Recognition lit in the eyes; they burned with unrestrained distain. The shadow turned into a fist that flew past Chloe's head. She was speeding away, the darkness lumbering after her.

"Leave me alone!" called the rasping voice as the creature bounced off walls. Pictures crashed to the floor. With a wave a cabinet full of figurines flew at her, propelled by long streams of darkness. Chloe screamed. She was down the hall. A clock smashed to the ground just behind her. She was in her conservatory. Like smoke hitting glass, the thing pooled and swirled at the steps. Fear flickered through those burning coals. Chloe sank chest deep into the floor where the well was. In a flash the thing was gone. Chloe wept.

It took several days before Chloe left her sanctuary. When she returned to the rest of the house, the first thing that caught her attention was that nothing had been cleaned. The shattered clock and broken cases still littered the hall. In the other rooms, everything seemed untouched. After a week, Chloe began to wonder if Mrs. Sellers or anyone was ever going to return. She wandered through the artifacts and broken detritus. She hated the thing that skulked upstairs, hated Edgar. She was angry with the workmen who disturbed it. She was angry that she was alone again.

Mrs. Sellers never returned. After a month different men came in to move a lot of the antiques out. They were almost finished when Chloe heard them on the stairs. Anguished moments passed as she tried to decide between helping and safety. Any moment now they would wake him up. She could already feel the atmosphere chill. She couldn't let them be attacked. She didn't know if it was possible, but she was sure she couldn't let the workers get hurt. Judging by the damage caused the last time she had encountered the malevolence, she was sure he would try. Making a decision, she appeared at the bottom of the stairs.

"You must leave," she called. Three frightened faces peered around a corner looking down at her. Relief washed over her. "You need to come downstairs," she beckoned, motioning them to come to her.

"Don't go down there!" one of the men cried. "She will pull you to hell."

"She wants to kill us," another shouted, disappearing from view.

"Go back to the grave!" called the third.

"No! Wait, what?" Chloe was confused and annoyed. Their shouting was going to wake him. "Wait, you need to..." Her explanation was drowning in the yells of the men. Without warning a porcelain figurine flew through Chloe's chest, smashing behind her. Now she was angry. "Fine! You don't want to listen to me?" A satisfied smile crossed her face before she cursed herself. The slamming of a door followed by heavy footfalls turned all faces to the far end of the hall. "Well, now you've done it." She frowned.

Screams filled the upstairs. The men were at the top looking between Chloe and the unfurling shadow. It took her a moment to realize why they were not retreating. It was because of her. They were terrified to come near her. Quickly she hid herself. With their path obstructed, the men still didn't budge. Not until the first man tumbled down the steps did his fellows follow. Chloe could see the hand imprint, red on the face of the fallen. His comrades pulled him to his feet. In a daze they dragged him as they ran from the house. Staying hidden in the shadows Chloe gasped as the shadows flew to the door throwing it wide. Everything that wasn't original to the house began to shoot through the opening, smashing and splintering on the walk and lawn. The screams of rage mixed with the violence of the purge sent Chloe back to her safe place. After a couple of hours, the smashing and crashing stopped. It was replaced with the sounds of furniture being slid around.

Again it took a few days before Chloe ventured back into the main part of the house. She was surprised to find all of the original furnishing back in place, covered in sheets to keep the dust off. Then she watched as those sheets change from white to gray as the years wore on. She wandered through the old house feeling alone, cut off from the world outside. Rarely did anyone set foot through the door. Occasionally she would see children through the windows; they would point at her and run away or throw rocks. She stopped looking out after that. Words the men had said stuck with her. They blamed and feared her.

The next time the boards came off the windows, Chloe was less interested in what was happening. Every time someone would come to make a change or look at the house, she would ignore them. With every visit all would be quiet until they reached the upstairs bedroom. Then it would all start again. She would hear them scream, hear them running down the stairs, out the door. Occasionally they would scream about the gray girl, the evil ghost, and she knew they didn't differentiate between her and what had was now Edgar or remnants of his worse traits.

Several experts came to the house. Mediums, researchers, and ghost hunters all came to find the gray girl. They would hear her weeping. They would try to make contact with her, but she didn't respond. She was in hell. She couldn't figure out what she had done to end up here, trapped with the man who had ended her life. When the intruders would finally make it upstairs, Chloe was happy. They would open the bedroom, and Edgar's hate would send them running for the hills. He would then rage through the empty halls, screaming to be left alone. She did her best to accommodate. She hated him. When he was near, she felt that hatred grow. It scared her to the point that she rarely emerged from the conservatory anymore. It got so bad that she would do whatever she could to drive people away before they woke him. She knew she was the only ghost they blamed. She hated them all now. She felt the anger, and it frightened her. She did not want to become what Edgar was.

It came to pass that Chloe rarely wandered or appeared. When the people would come, she would stay hidden. It came to the point where only children would sneak in on dares, or teens looking for a secluded place. She would remain hidden unless they threatened the house in some way or tried to go up the stairs. She had made it very difficult to access the stairs, blocking it with furniture and knocking out flashlights and candles of the would-be adventurers.

Boards covered the windows, and a fence enclosed the yard. Even the children stopped coming. Chloe avoided the rest of the house. She was stuck forever in the home of the man who had killed her. Sometimes she would fall to the anger. She had destroyed all of the mirrors. She could see herself in them, forever young and alone. The violence of her death did not mark her features. It was the injustice of it. Her only sin was refusing a ride. This gave him the right to run her down, shatter her body, and take her from her family, then trap her eternally with him in his home, forever fearing his presence.

Chloe sat alone on the battered settee letting the tears flow; anger and sorrow streamed down her face. Edgar was to blame for all of this. He got to live his life...She didn't know how long he had lived or how he had died. She didn't even know what year it was. She had been thrown down a well, fought to return to the surface, only to be trapped, while he most likely had lived a long and happy life to die and leave his evil behind. It was too much to bear. On top of all of that, there were people in her house. People she did not want in the house. Anger burst forth, she was on her feet, arms outstretched. The crashing of an ugly marble bust brought three men running. She stood pointing at them as they skidded to a halt.

"Get out of my house!" she boomed.

1947

"Oh look, the big war hero come to visit the lesser relations, huh?" Edgar slurred. Richard stood in the middle of the filthy front room, his tidy appearance and pressed dress uniform in distinct contrast to Edgar's disheveled one.

"I have heard the mill is not being very productive. That is not acceptable." Richard spoke calmly.

"Not acceptable!" Edgar shouted. "Not acceptable! You want to know what is not acceptable?" He struggled to rise off the tall wingback chair, the same chair his father used to sit in and look at his son with contempt. "What is not acceptable is Father left to everything to you." He shook his head knowing he wasn't making the most sense. "All I got was that failing mill and this tired old house. And that"—he pointed an accusing finger at Richard—"is probably because you couldn't be bothered with it. I've heard all about your fine house in Pittsburgh, though I have never been invited." Edgar grabbed an empty crystal glass, put it to his lips, noticed it was empty, and threw it across the room. Richard just sighed as the glass shattered. Then he spared Edgar a look of disappointment, so reminiscent of their father that Edgar shouted, "Don't! Don't you dare look at me like that!" He grabbed a bottle from the sideboard. Taking a long pull on the bottle, he turned back to his brother. "Why the hell are you still wearing that?" He pointed to the uniform.

"Because I am still in the army." Richard rubbed the bridge of his nose. "Look, I came here to tell you I have hired a manager for you." He ignored Edgar's look of disgust. "I know you can handle things." He raised a hand to halt the brewing protest. "I just want to help you get through this rough patch. He will be here on Monday." He grabbed a glass from the sideboard, took the bottle from Edgar, and poured a generous amount of the amber liquid. He ignored the murderous look on his brother's face. Handing back the bottle, he continued. "I hope you haven't had any more...troubles since I have been gone." The color drained from Edgar's face.

"No." Edgar slowly placed the bottle next to Richard's still half-full glass. "I don't go out much anymore."

"Ah, keep close to home then. Good."

"I don't want any more troubles." Edgar ran his hand over his face. "I can still see their faces." His trembling hand was reaching for the bottle. He closed his eyes. "The girl on the road, the one in the woods, the one by the lake. I'm haunted by them every day. I swear I see the one in the woods some nights. She is just standing there pointing at the house." He was swallowing large gulps of whiskey. "I was at the lake, and I swear I could see her face under the water. They are after me."

Richard laid a hand on Edgar's shoulder. "That is just your imagination. No one is after you."

"I don't know how much longer I can do it." Tears ran down Edgar's face. "They are always there, day and night. I have to get away from them." He took another drink. "Sometimes I think I should just go to the police, tell them everything." He turned to look into Richard's eyes. "Should I do that?"

"Now, now, brother of mine, you know you can't do that. If you tell anyone, it will be the ruin of the family name. Plus, you will get me into trouble for helping you," Richard explained.

"But I just can't take the guilt." Edgar wept.

"Listen, I have to leave the country for a while," Richard explained soothingly, his hands on Edgar's shoulders. "I have been deployed to someplace in Asia—Korea, I think it's called." Releasing his brother he opened another bottle and handed it over. Edgar drank greedily. "Just wait until I get back, and we will go to the police together. We'll explain what happened." He sipped his drink. "I mean the one walked in front of the car, the other was in the woods, and then the last one drowned on her own. Accidents. We just say you panicked or found them dead. It's not like"—he finished the glass—"you even remember killing them." Edgar moaned and wept harder, sinking down into the high back chair. "I ship out tomorrow, and Lawrence will be here on Monday to learn the ropes at the mill. Make sure he knows everything he needs to. OK?" Richard placed his cap smartly on his head. Edgar sniffed softly. He took another drink. Richard wasn't sure Edgar would even remember their talk.

Edgar spent the rest of the weekend in a haze of booze and guilt. Monday found him red-rimmed-eyed and shaky in his office. A knock at the door drew his attention. "Good morning, Edgar. My name is Lawrence Snowden; I believe Richard told you I was coming."

Edgar eyed the stranger with disgust. "My name is Mr. Davis. I don't care how friendly of terms you are on with my brother. I demand the respect of my employees." The look Lawrence returned was one of pleasantness, but his eyes were full of malevolence.

"Yes, sir. My apologies." Lawrence gave a short bow. "The last organization I worked for was a bit less formal, see."

Edgar snorted his disapproval. Shouting over Lawrence, he called for a weasel-faced man named Carl to show Lawrence around. Carl made no effort to show his contempt. As far as he was concerned, Edgar already had an assistant, and it was him. He played cards with Edgar and drank with him almost every afternoon. The other workers at the mill were more than happy to tell Lawrence about it after the second week he was there.

Carl and Edgar made it evident they did not like the new interloper or his ideas for the mill. After a month of—what Edgar deemed unnecessary—costly improvements, he had had it with the amount of money being spent. He was sitting in his office fretting over the numbers when shouting interrupted his thoughts. The bottle in his fist slowly sank to the desk as he rose to his feet. His anger was building with each step toward the door. He swung it wide to be greeted by Lawrence and Carl shouting at each other. Many of the workers had stopped to watch the altercation. Edgar was ready to let the shouting run its course until Carl threw a punch. It missed Lawrence, barely. Immediately people intervened, and Edgar had to do something. He hated having to do things.

"That is enough! Both of you, in my office now!" he bellowed. "As for the rest of you..." He pointed an accusing finger. "Get back to work." He turned running almost nose to nose with Lawrence. Carl was already in Edgar's office.

"I think this turn of events would make your brother very unhappy. Very unhappy indeed, especially if I were to tell him how you and your little friend there liked to spend so much time alone together." Lawrence smiled. Edgar had taken a step back. The intonation was clear.

"There is nothing of that sort going..." Edgar began.

"Oh, good to know. I'm sure Richard will be happy to hear that. He is ever so concerned about his brother." The smile turned cruel. "He hopes that your—how should we put this?— indiscretions have not moved on to more...unnatural desires," Lawrence whispered. Several eyes watched from behind machinery. Edgar grabbed Lawrence by the arm, hauling him to the office. He slammed the door so hard the glass cracked.

"I don't know what started it, but it is done," Edgar shouted at the two men. Carl cowered under the rage; Lawrence looked bored. Edgar dropped his voice to what he hoped was a deadly calm. Staring right into Lawrence's cold gray eyes, he spoke very clearly. "Carl is my floor manager, not you. That is all he is."

Lawrence looked over at Carl's sneering face and shrugged. "Good to know. I mean what two never-married men carrying on alone in this office get up to? Well, you can see how that causes rumors." The effect this had on Carl was as Lawrence had hoped.

"I...I...What? No, I was married. She died before the war," Carl choked out.

"Died, did she? I heard she ran off with a soldier and is living happily in Cleveland." Lawrence smiled at the pain he had just caused. "And as we know from Edgar's luck, women are just *dying*"—he emphasized the word—"to meet him. Or was it to get away from him?"

Edgar stumbled around his desk, nearly falling into his chair. His hands shook. It took a couple of attempts to speak through his cracking voice. Carl looked confused. "I think we should continue this discussion later. Over dinner perhaps? Yes, you both will come to my home at seven tonight, and we will figure out how to make this arrangement work for all parties involved." Edgar finished puffing himself up, trying to recapture the stature of the man in charge. "Right. So, out!" He pointed to the door. "Get back to work, and don't let me catch you two fighting," he shouted as Carl slunk from the room. Lawrence gave that short bow and smiled as he left, closing the door behind him. Edgar wiped the sweat from his forehead. He slowly opened the desk drawer, pulling the thick cloth-wrapped item out putting it in his empty lunch box. The bottle it had previously contained lay empty under the desk.

Edgar made a call to the housekeeper. She was to prepare an elegant meal for him and his guests. When the appointed time

rolled around, he was not disappointed. Nervously he had
waited, so he had already had a few calming drinks before his
guests arrived. Each brought a bottle for their host, and they
had wine with dinner. After the plates had been cleared away,
Edgar sent the housekeeper home. He sat in the parlor drinking
scotch and smoking cigars with his guests discussing how they
could all work together. That was what he remembered they
were talking about.

Now the room was dark. He was still in his clothes, but he
was no longer in the parlor. Cold sweat broke out across his
face. "No, no, not again," he whimpered. Two voices talking low
and quickly caught his attention. A light from the hall was
flickering. Through his stupor he could make out Lawrence and
Carl having an intense discussion. "Waz...wazgone on?" he
slurred. Lawrence quickly hushed Carl.

"Had a bit too much, I'm afraid. We had to put you to bed.
Last place they'll look, I'm sure," Lawrence explained. Carl
sniggered. "Was awfully nice of you to bring along this fine
weapon." Lawrence was showing the gun Edgar had brought
home from the office. He had intended to use it on Lawrence,
letting Carl take the blame. His drinking had ruined that plan.
Edgar tried desperately to recall whether he had told them of
the plan. "Oh, don't worry, I'm sure you had plans for this, and I
did bring my own but when an opportunity presents itself."
Lawrence was aiming the weapon at Edgar. Carl was easing
backward away. "I had planned to have this look like a suicide,
but after conferring with dear Carl, I think we have a better
plan."

Edgar tried to raise himself, tried to protest, barter, beg, but
all he could do is mutter, "Why?"

Lawrence laughed. "Because you are a liability, ole boy." His smile was barely hidden in the shadows. "A problem that needs to be fixed, a loose end to tie up."

Looking past Lawrence, Edgar blinked, trying to bring the picture into focus. He smiled weakly. Behind the shooter stood Carl, his longtime confidant and pal. Carl held a gun of his own. Edgar smiled; his head swiveled as he tried to stay awake. They'll tell the police it was self-defense, and it was. Edgar laughed. He pointed and laughed until the laugh died in his throat. It seemed more like a pop than a bang. Edgar had expected louder. It hurt to breathe. His shirt was wet. He looked up at Lawrence silhouetted in the door. A louder bang, and Lawrence crumpled to the floor. Now Edgar could see Carl. In the hall a blue haze of smoke lingered.

"Looks like you'll be gone soon enough," Carl sneered as he wiped the gun clean. He was at Lawrence's body. Edgar couldn't see what Carl was doing. He was weak and cold. Carl reappeared holding Edgar's gun. He was at Edgar's side now. Edgar's blurry vision was dimming. "I have put up with you too long," Carl whispered. "Oh the things I know and the money I am being paid to keep it quiet." He leaned closer to Edgar's ear. "I know who actually killed those girls." He giggled. "You are such a patsy." Edgar felt something cold, metal, and heavy in his hand. Carl was at the door, his face half-illuminated from the hall. "God, I have hated your sorry drunken ass for so long. I am finally rid of you."

Edgar was dying. Lawrence had shot him, and then Carl had shot Lawrence. Edgar's mind was spinning. What did Carl mean he knew who killed the girls? The tunnels were closing in on his vision. Didn't Edgar kill them? He was going to hell now. The light faded.

UNEXPECTED

"Get out of my house!" Chloe cried, rising off the floor. She pointed accusingly at them. Floating near the ceiling, she looked down on the three men, two of which were crouched, holding each other, fear gleaming in their huge eyes.

"No!" Alex shouted.

The word sunk in. "What?" Chloe replied, letting her arm fall to her side.

"What?" stammered Arnold and Aaron in unison.

"I said no," replied Alex calmly. "Why should we leave? We bought this house. Who are you to tell us to leave?" Arnold was pulling on Alex's sleeve.

"But this is my house..." Chloe faltered. Technically it wasn't really hers. She was bound to it and couldn't leave, so she decided. "Yes! This *is* my house! You will leave now." She attempted to recover menacingly.

"If you are who I think you are," Alex continued in a calm voice, "you didn't own this place." He looked over at his brother and father, who were slowly inching toward the door. "This was, judging by your appearance, Edgar Davis's house when..." Now it was Alex's turn to falter as the air turned frigid. His breath clouded his vision of the specter for a second. A deep purple glowed from her eyes; red fringed her outline; anger pulsated from her very core. Alex stumbled back a step.

"Get *out!*" Chloe cried. Potted plants crashed to the ground. Dead leaves swirled around the men, chasing them out into the hall. The wind and noise followed them to the front door and through. They didn't stop running until they were back in the trucks. Gravel spit, and tires screamed as they headed down the driveway.

Chloe's anger subsided. She laughed. It had been fun scaring them. Her smile faded quickly while regret slowly seeped in. She should have asked what had happened to her family. She should have found out what had happened to Edgar. Where were her mother and brother now? Silently she cursed her actions as she surveyed the detritus of the conservatory. She returned to her solitary mourning on the bench.

A day went by with Chloe wandering aimlessly through the empty halls. She was absently poking at an old vase she had never liked when she heard the front door slam. Footfalls echoed down the hall through to the conservatory. She ignored it. If they didn't find her, then maybe they'd go away. She floated on until another idea hit her. If they didn't find her, they might never leave. Swearing and annoyed, she swooped down to the conservatory. There was the young man who had questioned her bent over the remains of the marble bust. As he stood something flashed in his hand.

Chloe stopped. She was staring at the object in the hand of the wide-eyed man, who stood rooted to the spot. Her own hand stretched out of its own accord, reaching for the small diamond earring. "My mother gave that to me," she whispered. It passed warmly through her fingers. She could feel the love of her mother in it.

"Are you Chloe...Chloe Miller?" Alex whispered. He held the earring out, so she could still caress it. He could feel her feather-light ghostly touch on his fingers.

"I was," she sighed. The memories the small piece of jewelry brought flooded her mind. She was laughing while cooking with her mother. She felt the joy of playing with her brother, the pride she had helping her father work on the old tractors. She remembered the house, the smell of it, the warmth and love in the place. She remembered her room, her books, and her friends. She missed all of it so much it hurt. Large pearly tears leaked from her opal eyes.

Alex could feel the sorrow emanating from her. To his surprise an aura of the palest blue surrounded her. Something about her drew him. His hands moved of their own free will. It felt right. It was as if he had to do this. He stepped forward; Chloe recoiled. He paused. "This belongs with you," he said, taking another step toward her again. She moved farther back, yet her eyes never left the diamond.

Her sad smile, the way she cocked her head, made his heart ache. "You should have this back." Then it hit him. "Why is this here?" She was now looking at him confused. "I mean um, wow." He rubbed his neck, not sure how to proceed. "I mean wasn't this...buried with you?" He closed his eyes, frustrated at his own insensitivity. "No one ever found you," he muttered.

Alex was shocked at the soft voice. "I'm down there." She pointed to a place on the floor. "He threw me in there."

"What, in the concrete?"

"No, there was a well." Her voice trembled.

"I don't...I mean...shit...didn't Edgar hit you with his car?"

She looked into his eyes. He could see she was stunned. "You know?" she asked.

"I guess Granddad was right," Alex whispered.

"Granddad? Who is your Granddad?" she asked softly, moving closer to study his face. "You look familiar." She leaned her head from side to side, examining his features. A smile spread across her face but was quickly chased away. "You look like Rupert, Rupert Holt." She was backing away again.

"He was my granddad." He hesitated, backing away. He wanted to keep her from leaving. "He never stopped trying to find out what happened to you." Alex's hand passed through her shoulder. It felt like passing through cold water buy dry. He looked at his hand. There was nothing different about it.

For Chloe it felt warm and somehow comforting. "No," she cried, backing away. Rupert was dead. Rupert got married, had kids and grandkids, and one of them was here talking to her. She was happy for him and so angry at him as well. "We were going to go..."

"To the winter dance together. He asked you right before you died."

"Yes." Her back was to him.

"I read his journal. He was so excited when you accepted."

"He was?" she whispered.

"Yeah. He was so worried when you disappeared. Then when he knew you...you weren't coming back. He was heartbroken."

They stood in silence for a long time. Alex didn't know what else to say. It was getting uncomfortable. He was about to make his exit when she asked, "Was he happy?"

"He was always laughing and joking. That is what I remember most about him." Alex smiled at the memory. "He named his plane after you. In the war."

"Which war? I read about several since I died," she inquired.

"Oh right, um, the Second World War."

"My dad fought in the first one." She thought for a second. "They called it the war to end all wars, but Dad said another one was coming." She remembered sitting in the kitchen, her father reading the paper talking about Europe. "He said it was only a matter of time." She recalled the look her father gave over the paper at her brother was one of fear. "Do you know if my brother fought in the war?"

"I'm sorry, I don't." Silence extended like a chasm between them. Her attention was back on the small sparkling stone. He followed her gaze, remembering it was in his hand. He held it out to her. That was when he noticed a few things about her he hadn't before. There were marks on her neck. They looked like a thin burn. He could see one ear contained an earring; the other was blurred and torn. She was also missing a shoe. He barely noticed this last aspect as she floated about an inch above the ground.

Not sure what he was doing, he pulled the back from the earring. He took a step toward her. She backed away fearful. "I'm not going to hurt you. I, I guess I don't know." He held out the jewelry.

"Will that work?" she asked. He voice was quiet, timid, and scared.

"I seriously have no idea." They looked at each other for a moment. He smiled at her; she smiled back. He reached slowly forward. She pulled her hair from her ear. It floated like water through the air. The ear became clearer as he reached for it. It enveloped the earring. The ear became whole yet still ghostly. The small diamond sparked briefly before it became like the one in her other ear.

For Chloe the touch of the small piece of old jewelry was incredible. The warmth of her mother's love filled her. "Thank you for returning this to me," she whispered. Chloe felt some of her sadness, anger, and pain evaporate in the warmth. She smiled sadly at him.

"Your eyes were blue," he said, astonished.

"Yes, they are...were," she replied, shocked. "How did you know?"

"I can see them, pale but there seems to be..." Alex searched for the words. "More to you?" He looked her over. She took on the appearance of something like an old faded photograph now. Not quite clear but better, more substantial.

"I don't understand," she stated, looking at her hands. There was more there, but she was far from solid.

Alex was pacing as Chloe inspected her hands and arms. "How are you here?" he finally asked. "I thought ghosts only lived..." Sheepishly he looked at her. "You know what I mean, stayed where they died." He thought for a moment. "My Granddad thought you got hit by a car."

She sunk onto the settee. He joined her there. The look on her face was so sad. Alex didn't want to upset her. He meant to ask if she was OK, but instead she had the first question. "How long have I been dead?"

"I think about seventy years." He moved to lay a hand on hers, hesitated, and returned it to his own lap. The silence filled the room until it was deafening. "*Your shoe!*" he cried. "You're missing a shoe!"

Chloe sprang away when he yelled but now was looking down to her feet. "Yes I lost it when..."

"When you were hit by a truck! Right?" Alex was on his feet. "Granddad found it. He said it was proof you got hit and didn't run away."

"My family thought I ran away?" The pain in her voice stabbed at Alex's heart.

"I...I don't know." He was pacing, muttering to himself. "If the earring did that, what would the shoe do?"

Chloe wasn't listening. "What happened to my family?" She was floating back and forth opposite to his pacing. "They can't have thought I ran away. Please, you have to find out what happened to my parents and my brother. You have to tell them I didn't run away." She was inches from him, pleading.

Alex was shocked. "I, um, OK. What is, was, whatever, your address?" He hesitated. "I'll find out."

"We lived at 3206 Arlington Road. My father was Eldon, mom was Sue, and my brother is Charlie."

He could see her slipping into sadness again. Fearing her response, he tentatively asked. "And...um...jeez, this is a weird thing to say...um." He fidgeted with his fingers, flipping them against his nails, a habit that drove his family crazy. "Why haven't you gone to check on them?"

Chloe explained what happened when she tried to leave the house. Alex's brow furrowed in confusion. "I don't mean to be insensitive, but..." He hesitated. "Didn't you die on the road?" She cocked her head to look at him. "I mean why aren't you, um out..." He couldn't look her in the eye. "Why aren't you haunting where you died?"

She laughed softly without humor. "Oh, that is easy. I died here. Under the floor is a well. After he hit me, I didn't die. After he threw me down the well, I still didn't die. It wasn't until he caved in the well with explosives that I finally died."

Alex stood, transfixed in horror. "How could he do that?" he cried. "That is...how...I'm so sorry." Alex was sure he knew the answer to his next question. "Who...killed you?

The worry lines that had formed on her brow smoothed. "Oh that. That was Edgar Davis. His family used to own this house." She looked away.

Alex reached out to comfort her. To his horror, his hand passed into her shoulder. Quickly retracting it, he apologized. She stared at him, the look on her face unfathomable. "I've never been touched." She whispered, "Well, not since I died." Her laugh was light. "What was it like?"

"I don't know. It was...I felt your presence. I felt something like a resistance, but, I don't know, it was different." He cocked his head, trying to think of the best way to describe it. "What was it like for you?"

"Warm." Her eyebrows knitted as she struggled to find the words. "Nice, I guess?" She shrugged. Concern crossed her face as she watched emotions race across his face. It finally spread into a grin.

"Well, we've both had a first. You're the first ghost I've touched, and I'm the first to touch you as a ghost." The smile began to slide from his face as she didn't reply. "I'm—that wasn't right—I'm a jerk. I'm sorry."

She glared at him. The look she wore caused him to recoil. "Don't you go telling stories about me like I'm your ghost girlfriend or something. It was just a touch, nothing more. The other ghosts don't approve of inter-life-and-death couples." The corner of her mouth twitched. She couldn't hold it and began to laugh at his discomfort.

"You are not funny," he said in relief, joining her in a laugh. The smile on his face changed. "I just thought of something. Maybe since your earring was returned to you..." He was on his feet again. "Maybe you can leave now."

A cautious smile crossed her face. "Maybe?" Alex never wanted to witness what happened next ever again. She told him she was able to make it farther than she had ever before. It had been encouraging until the extent of what happened to her showed itself. The horror and pain she had to have endured tore at him. When he left her sitting on the settee that night, she had stopped crying at least. He felt her suffering was his fault for even suggesting she try to leave.

RESEARCH

A few days later, found Alex was deep in the archives at the main public library branch. He had found records for the house at 3206 Arlington Road. The house had been sold in 1958. Alex found out it was sold after Eldon had died of a heart attack. It took him a while longer to find out what had happened to Sue. She had moved in with her sister after Eldon died. She had died in 1964. It took him a long time to find out what had happened to Charlie. He was only fourteen when Chloe had gone missing. Alex checked through military records, finding Charlie Miller there. He had been wounded in combat a couple of times, but there was nothing about being killed. He also hadn't returned to town.

"I'm still trying to find out what happened to your brother," Alex called over his shoulder. Chloe took the death of her parents hard. She knew they must be dead, but it still hurt more than she could have thought possible. Alex tried to comfort her. but felt useless in the end. He couldn't give her news of her brother or hold her while she cried. With nothing else to do, he turned to research.

Charlie had been with the marines in the Pacific. After the war Alex found out that Charlie had remained with the marines but also went to school to become a lawyer. It was during the Korean War that Alex found more information on Charlie. Lieutenant Charlie Miller was attached to the judge advocate general's office in Seoul starting in 1952. He had an exemplary record as a soldier and as a lawyer.

It was during this time that he represented the prosecution against a Colonel Davis, who was accused of destroying a village without orders or evidence of being combative. Alex found that Charlie had been taken off the case due to his knowledge of the Davis family and a police report from 1938. It was a complaint by Edgar against Alex's grandfather, and it mentioned that Charlie was also involved.

Alex searched for the outcome of the trial. He was not surprised to find all charges against Davis were dropped. All evidence disappeared while all the soldiers who were to testify were killed in an ambush. Alex got lost in tracking Davis until more charges were filed against him in Vietnam in 1967. Again Charlie's name came up in the JAG office. Alex stared at the picture attached to the article. Charlie showed every one of the years since Korea. Richard Davis showed none. He looked as he had during the first trial. Searching back through records, Alex found Davis had been in Europe and the Pacific during World War II.

Alex looked away from the screen, rubbing his eyes. A small town in France had been completely wiped out. Davis's unit had been suspected in the killings, but no proof could be collected because the Nazis retook the area briefly. "God, I thought Edgar was a murderous bastard." Alex sighed. He scrolled down the page. He gagged and spit out his coffee. There was a picture of Richard. Alex opened a new tab, recalling the article from Korea, then another for Vietnam. Richard never changed.

Alex had to find Charlie. He was sure Charlie knew something about how Richard seemed to be involved in horrible atrocities yet never seemed to get convicted and never seemed to age. Continuing to search, Alex was finally able to find Charlie retired to a town sixty miles away. *Problem is he'd be like ninety now,* Alex thought.

The next day Alex drove the miles and was now looking at an older home in good repair. The wheelchair access was very well built. "He'd been a lawyer; I guess even military lawyers get paid well," he told the mailbox. Taking in a breath to gather his courage, Alex walked up to the door. Exhaling and not having a clue what to say, he rang the bell.

"May I help you?" A woman with eyes Alex recognized answered the door. She was older, in her sixties, but her intense blue eyes were unmistakable.

"I, uh, hi, my name is Alex Holt, and I—"

"Let me stop you right there," she interrupted. "I am not buying anything, and you seriously need to work on your delivery." The door was closing.

Not sure what to do, Alex began to panic. "I am looking for Charlie Miller; is he home?"

"Sorry, you just missed him." The woman sighed. "By about two years."

"I came about his sister," Alex called to the millimeters left of opening.

One of those blue eyes became visible. "What do you know about Cindy?"

"Wait, what? Cindy? No, Chloe is her name." Alex looked down, scratching his head. Confusion bounced around in his brain. Who was he talking to? He was so distracted, he hadn't noticed the door was open.

"Have you seen her?" The question caused Alex to pause.

"Yes." Alex stumbled over his words. "Well, I met Chloe. I mean, well..."

"Dad was sure he saw her." The woman stood aside to let Alex in. "He named me after her." She held out a hand to him. "Chloe Zielsky. Please come in."

1967

"Do you really think you can do any better this time?" Richard Davis's muttering whisper was drowned out by the heavy traffic of the city. "You see, I am not even behind bars. No one remembers seeing me at the village." He spoke now into his glass of expensive whiskey. Smiling over the glass, he slowly placed it on the table. "What do you expect to prove by this anyway?" He sniffed. "You will be barred from pursuing this case as well."

After a salute and a request to join his superior, Lieutenant Colonel Charlie Miller accepted his own drink with a thanks to the waitress. He hadn't spoken a word since laying the folder on the table before Colonel Davis and ordering the drink. Miller, for his part, sipped his drink, savoring the cold of the water. Looking up from the glass that was leaving a ring of condensation on the white tablecloth of the barely air conditioned hotel bar, he smiled. "You're looking very well, Colonel."

Richard was taken aback by the comment. Charlie continued, "Myself, I can't get used to this heat." He wiped his forehead with one of the napkins. Seeing the look on his companion's face, he apologized. "I am sorry. I did not have the upbringing you did. Of course, you know that." He sipped his drink. "You must be used to this heat, I would think."

"And why would I be used to this heat?" Richard asked, his lips barely moving.

"Oh, nothing, I just assumed you'd be used to this hellish heat..." Charlie smiled. "You know, from your service in Korea and elsewhere." He looked at the ice water, frowned, and waved the waitress over. "I think I'll have a bourbon, please, on ice. Colonel, would you like another?"

"I don't think you could afford this." Richard smiled apologetically.

"You're probably right." Charlie took another sip of water again. "What's it cost? An arm and a leg? Or just your soul?" He laughed as he smiled at the waitress as she placed the bourbon on the table. "Might not be just one, depending on the vintage, right?" He swirled his new drink. "Something from the thirties might cost you three souls, if you could, of course, get ahold of the devil's liquid back then." Charlie did not look up from his glass, a satisfied smile on his face. He could see Richard's posture stiffen. "Then what? Once a decade one might pay a price to enjoy the, um, benefits of the drink?" Charlie was now looking straight into Richard's eyes. He stared back. The deep brown of his reflected Charlie's light blue.

"You know that was a very...odd...analogy." Richard smiled, holding a look of pleasant confusion. "I'm not sure I follow your meaning, though."

Charlie saw the smile did not reach Richard's eyes. In those eyes he saw, anger? Hatred? Leaning in close, his voice was barely above a whisper. "Oh, I think I know the whole story now." He finished his drink. Leaving the folder in front of Richard, he left the bar. Richard watched him go then stared at the folder as if it had offended him. Finally curiosity got the better of him. Richard opened the folder expecting to see photos of the destroyed village. He remembered the charred corpses, the screams of the children as mothers were violated and killed before their eyes. He flipped to the first page. It contained three names along with a year, then another name, and another. "Damn it, Edgar." He breathed.

Richard retired to his room at the hotel. The folder and its contents still smoldered in the trash can. He inspected his uniform. He was very proud of the ribbons and medals. He had been wearing a uniform since 1941. He liked it. He was in line to become a general just like his great-great-grandfather had been in the Civil War. He adjusted the cap.

Charlie had found what he needed. One way or another, he was going to get the information out of Richard. Edgar, while dead, would never be tried for the murders, but maybe they would look for other's involvement. Even if they didn't, the stain on the family name may keep him from the promotion.

It took a while to understand what he was seeing. The RPG fired from the shoulder of the man dressed in black. The explosion on the third floor of the four-story hotel, another man ran into the lobby firing his AK, then the explosion. Charlie lay in the street, ears ringing. Blood-covered patrons staggered out of the hotel lobby. Charlie stumbled into the debris. The waitress from the day before lay in two pieces, an ocean of blood still spreading between them. The clatter of gunfire outside the hotel caused pockmarks to appear in the already-shattered room. Through the smoke and falling plaster, Charlie ran up the three flights, turned down the hall. Where Richard's room should have been there was daylight. A shoulder with a colonel's eagle lay in the hall. The top of a head still stuck in the hat. Charlie would not get his answers today.

Alex closed the journal as his phone rang. "Hello, Dad." He cringed. His host sipped her tea, watching him over her glasses. "I know, I know." He shrugged. "What, no! You can't sell it. No." Alex listened for a moment. "No, Dad, I can work something out. I can get her to let us do some work." A smile crossed his face. "Yes, I will ask her as soon as I get back to town." He paused to listen. "No, I am trying to figure out a way to help her." Alex smiled at Chloe across from him, feeling how odd it was to talk about her eponym in front of her. "Yeah, I know, yes...Love you, too, Pops." Alex hung up. "Sorry about that. Are there any more of these journals?"

Chloe smiled. "I have not looked at this stuff in years. My father spent a lot of time trying to find out what Edgar had done that allowed Richard his youthful looks." She left the room for a moment, returning with two large binders. "This is all his research. Please take it with you. Maybe you can find what he missed." The heavy books were in his hands. The door was held open for him, and he was on the porch. "I hope you find a way to let her rest." The door snapped shut.

Alex drove back home, his mind reeling with all he had read. It made no sense to him. Why did Charlie think Edgar had made a deal? A deal that benefited Richard. If Edgar had made a deal, it didn't work out so well for him. Alex decided he needed to know more about Richard, and the first person he was going to ask was someone who was alive when he was: Chloe.

BACK IN THE HOUSE

"I died eighty years ago. What is it like now?" Chloe asked, resuming her seat and patting the cushion next to her. "I'm glad we never had the atomic war...did we?"

Alex laughed. "No, we never had the nuclear war, came damn close a couple of times. We've had other wars, though." His smile slipped from his face at the thought of how many wars had occurred since she had passed.

"Are you all right?" she asked.

"Yeah, just got me thinking." He sighed. "All these years, and we still can't seem to get along in the world." His smile returned. "We have a lot of cool ways to communicate now." Pulling out his phone, he showed her the Internet, videos, photos, and messaging.

"Does anyone actually talk to each other?" she asked after he told her about text messages and e-mail.

Alex thought for a moment. "No, not really." She waited for him to continue. Alex tried to think of the best way to ask his question. "Listen, I need to ask you about...Richard and Edgar." He felt the weight hit the pit of his stomach as she turned from him. She was up and floating away in an instant. Alex found himself on his feet reaching out. Her transparent hair slipped through his fingers as she moved. "Wait, I'm sorry; I just need to understand. I learned some things, and they just don't make sense." Now it was Alex who turned away. "Listen, I uh..." He had decided to tell her about her brother. Now his stomach squirmed at the thought of telling her he was gone. *Then again not knowing could be worse,* he thought. Steeling himself, he shut his eyes, turned back to her direction, and spoke. "I found your brother." He heard her gasp but continued on. "He was already...gone when I got to his house."

"Where did he go? When was he going to be back? Did you tell him about me?" Chloe interrupted, her tone more excited with each question. A sudden gasp and her hands flew to cover her mouth. "Oh my, you meant he died."

He could only stutter as he watched the tears well up. She turned from him, shoulders shaking. It was with careful hands that he held her presence by the shoulders. She turned, his hands passing through her. He found an odd weight on his shoulders and neck. His arms encircled, pressing just enough not to pass into her. Tears flowed out onto his shoulder. To his surprise, the material became cold where she cried but remained dry. He did what he could to comfort her, wishing to help as well as reveling in the feeling of the wisps through his fingers as he ran them through the flow of her hair.

"Your heart is beating so fast," she remarked as her shoulders calmed from crying. "Mine hurts but doesn't beat anymore." She choked back a sob. Her hands were now on his chest. Her head turned to listen to the rhythm in his chest.

"Um, yeah. Well, I didn't get to tell you." He backed away, immediately missing the feeling of her. "I met your niece." Quickly he explained what he had discovered during his visit. She listened, making few remarks until the end.

"So he thought it was me haunting this place, but he never came to find out?" she asked as she wandered to a window.

"I think he hoped it wasn't you, and if he found out it was, it would confirm you were gone," he suggested. He decided to try again. "So what can you tell me about Richard?"

"Nothing really." She continued to stare through the filthy glass. "He was younger, handsome, and very well liked." She turned to face him. "From what I heard, nothing at all like

Edgar." She frowned. "I always understood there was a deep resentment by Edgar of his brother. Richard was smarter and much better with the ladies." She smirked, which turned to an ugly frown. "Edgar was mean, ugly, and crass. He was..." She glanced around, looking for the right word. "Not smart, a galoot, I guess." She was pacing now. "I did hear that Richard would often cover for Edgar. Like when Edgar got mad and damaged old Mr. Graham's wagon, Richard paid for a new one."

"So you think Edgar did something to help his brother out?" Alex asked.

Chloe frowned. "No. I really doubt it. Well, I don't know. I never believed in any of that stuff, but, well..." She motioned to herself. "I guess ghosts are real." Suddenly she yelped. Alex rushed to her, not sure what had surprised her. Chloe stared at him wide-eyed. "Their grandmother!" she cried.

"What, is she here?" He was staring all around trying to shield her.

Chloe passed right through him, turned to stare him in the eyes. "No, she isn't here." She laughed. "Such a gentleman to guard me from harm. Little hint, though." She winked at him. "I'm already dead. No, their grandmother was rumored to be a witch." She shook her head. "Until right now I never even thought of it."

"No shit? Really? A witch?"

"Language." Chloe blushed.

"Sorry."

1932

"Your father would not approve of you visiting me." The old woman's voice was harsh. "Even though he would not be where he is today without my help." She looked the visitor up and down through the crack in the door. The disgust on her face was not even attempted to be concealed.

"Yes Grandmother Raven. He has truly been wrong..."

"I may have given birth to that ungrateful whelp; that does not make us family," Raven hissed, opening the door slowly. "You want something from me? There is a price," she muttered, turning her back to him as he entered. She turned and looked him over again. Her bony hand emerged from beneath her filthy shawl. Her fingers rubbed the inexpensive fabric of his coat. "A price I doubt you could pay." She cackled.

"Listen, you old crone," he spat, dropping all civility. "I know more than you think I do; I am more than you think I am." Before he could explain, he was cut off.

"If you know so much, then why come seeking my help?" she demanded. "You and yours have done all you can to deny me, shun me, push me away. Now you insult me?" A ball of flame erupted in her hand. She tossed it from one hand to the other. "You would do well to leave now." Without further warning, flames sped across the room, exploding beside the man's head; he barely flinched.

The man was laughing now as he calmly advanced on Raven. "You cannot hurt me." He mocked her tone. "You will assist me."

"Young fool," she hissed as a flutter of wings erupted from the corner of the room. Black ravens emerged from the darkness. Like angry black darts, they flew at the man. The old woman's laughter urged their flight. Taking a step back, he reached into his pocket, quickly drawing out a small pouch. Pulling the string, he threw a powder into the air. The ravens burst into black dust. Coughing, the man brushed the dirt from his shoulder.

"That was a warning." Raven's voice betrayed a hint of fear. Blue flame simmered in her cupped hands. "This will destroy you."

Fast as lightning, his hands disappeared into his jacket again, pulling forth a vial containing a red liquid and a silver dagger. "You know what I have here." He held out the vial. "All I have to do it drop it."

The blue flames continued to crackle. "And if the bottle doesn't break?" Raven demanded.

"Then the blade of Baphoment will do the trick." He flicked the end of the dagger. A cut appeared on the old woman's face. "In all actuality, I don't actually need you." Another flick of the blade. Raven cried out as a deep cut appeared on her arm. "I really just need your books." Another flash of silver, another cry of pain. "Oh and blood, so maybe I do need you after all."

After the cries of agony died away in the night, red-black flames erupted through the circle, surrounding the star on the floor. Angry fire danced through the room, sending red-yellow light through the filthy windows of the old shack. The blaze tore through the already-crumbling roof. In the center of the inferno, a voice filled with menace and hate asked, "What is it you desire?"

Can We Work?

"So, their grandmother lived out in a shack in the woods while they lived here?" Alex marveled. "So what happened to her?" The shadows had grown long as they had been talking. Alex had no idea how long it had been.

"I don't know for sure. They say she died in a fire..." Chloe spoke slowly. Her eyes stared past Alex toward the door. Alex turned slowly. He was afraid of what he might see. There in the doorway was a shadow, tall and thin. Chloe was already gliding away. Alex could feel the pressure of her hand trying to pull him back. A scratching scurrying could be heard in the walls.

"What is that?" Alex whispered.

"It's Edgar, but he's never come in here before," Chloe whimpered.

"Um, Alex?" The shadow spoke softly. Aaron stepped into the light. "Dad and I would like to know if we can maybe do some work on the house now."

Alex was bent over, drawing deep breaths. In between nervous laughing, he tried to steady his watery legs. Chloe had melted into the wall. She was hiding from Aaron. "Chloe," Alex called. "It's OK. It's just my brother, Aaron. You can come out." Alex waited, but Chloe did not return.

"Was that her?" Aaron asked, staring at where he had last seen the girl.

"Yeah," was all Alex could think to say.

"Did you ask her?" Aaron whispered, grabbing Alex's arm.

"What?" Alex asked dumbfounded. He wasn't sure if Aaron meant about Edgar, or..."Oh, right, about the house."

Immediately he tried to calm Aaron, who was beginning to boil in frustration. "We kinda got sidetracked. I'll go ask her."

"You've been here for over two hours," Aaron shouted.

"Yeah, well. she has missed out on a lot, you know."

"Come on, man, we need to get moving on this. Dad sunk a ton into buying this place." Aaron was getting started on a rant. Normally Alex would head him off before things got too heated, but he was distracted. Chloe was nowhere to be seen. "Damn it, Alex. I'm talking to you."

"Yeah, and I'm not listening. You think you would've learned the signs by now." Alex pushed past his brother. "Not much I can do when you scared her off."

"I scared her off!" Aaron stormed. "You sure you didn't bore her to de…?"

"Dude."

Aaron and Alex stared at each other, the anger between them evaporating through awkward snickers. "Oh, man, I hope she didn't hear that," Aaron whispered.

"Naw, she is actually really cool about that stuff." Alex again swept the area, trying to find Chloe. "Hey, Chloe, I want you to meet my annoying older brother, Aaron." They waited.

SCRATCHING IN THE DARK

Something scurried off to Chloe's left. There was something about it that frightened her. This was not a rat; she was not afraid of rats or mice. They had been her only company for many years. This was something else, something evil. Not sure why she was pursuing it instead or retreating to the conservatory, Chloe continued on. Passing through plaster, studs, and plumbing, she followed the clicking claws behind the walls. The closer she got, the more she became aware the creature's squeaking and growling was more than just noise. It was speaking.

"He is asking too many questions," it croaked. "Master needs to know. Too many questions." Through the creature's panting and scratching, she could tell the voice was now moving above her. If it went upstairs, she would be too close to Edgar. The moment of indecision was smashed as the creature spoke again. "The boy must go. Yes, yes, the whole family. But should I kill them, Master?" Years of dirt and dust fell through Chloe as she sped after the voice. She couldn't let it hurt Alex. The thought surprised her.

Kerlvin had heard them talking in the conservatory. They were talking about things that were not meant to be discussed. It was why he was here, to keep the secrets, and the boy was learning too many. Kerlvin ran, hunched over and small, through the wall. He liked the sound his claws made as he ascended the pipe to the second floor. The closer he got to the aperture, the more complete he felt. He had been away for a long time. Slowing, he began muttering to himself, "I could let him find out. Then maybe I could finally go home." He sat on a cross beam, tapping a slender black talon against his inky lip.

Chloe pressed into the wall. Half-in and half-out of the plaster, she stood watching. The creature she pursued was sleek, scaly, and the color of midnight. It adjusted unfurling leathery wings that wrapped back around its body like a cape. It continued to tap its mouth and mutter. Chloe could not make out what it was saying. Words like, *kill* and *death* grabbed her attention. Very slow and cautiously, she rose inch by inch closer to where it sat. Straining, she tried to make out what it was saying. Suddenly its head spun in her direction. Red eyes burned as a hiss exposed the glistening white pointed teeth. In a flash it scampered up a pipe, the rust flying, claw marks leaving shiny trails in the metal. Had she been seen? Chloe followed as fast as she dared until she knew there was no reason to pretend.

The chase stopped. Crouched, ready to strike, Kerlvin sat just out of her reach. "Why does the dead girl chase Kerlvin?" Chloe heard as red eyes glowered down at her. Without waiting for an answer, a black tail slashed the air as it disappeared through an impossibly small hole in the wall. Chloe was alone and hesitant. Cursing under her breath, she followed him, materializing in a hall that stood thick with disuse. Several feet away stood the demon Kerlvin. He stood two feet tall on crouched legs. His claws ripped at the battered runner, his small hands held out in front of his red-black body, the fingers flexing. Blood-red eyes stared at her while the long dagger of a tongue flicked across his lips. Leathery black wings erupted from his back. Dust swirled as they flapped. "What does the dead girl want of Kerlvin?"

Chloe wondered how her stomach could be so twisted while she knew she didn't have one, how her knuckles cracked as she twisted her fingers. She was so consumed by these thoughts, she did not realize the creature was staring at her. His head cocked, brows knitted, he watched her movements. Dropping her hands, she spoke in a tone much braver than she felt. "Who are you?" she demanded. He blinked back at her, his eyes becoming black pools reflecting her pearly appearance. "What are you doing here?" she shouted.

Immediately Kerlvin held a spindly finger to his lips. "Don't arouse Edgar," he hissed.

"Aren't you Edgar?" she demanded yet in softer tones. She thought for a moment, studying the small devil. "If you're not Edgar, would that mean you're just a foul little demon from hell?

"I am not Edgar, dead girl. I am Kerlvin. I am not a foul little demon; I am a grand demon," he explained grumpily. His wings slumped; a sneer curled his lip. "Well, I am a minor demon," he corrected in a mutter.

"Are you Edgar's...pet?"

This question earned Chloe a glare that reignited the glowing red eyes that were barely visible through the cloud of dust swirling in the wake of Kerlvin's wings. "I am no one's pet, dead girl! Edgar is my pet. He was given to me," he spat angrily.

Hushing Kerlvin, she hissed back, "My name is Chloe!"

"I care not for what your name is. I care only about how much longer it will be." The demon growled as his feet touched down in another swirl of dust.

"What do you mean, how much longer? Who gave him to you?"

"Questions, questions, too many questions. Dead girl asks too many questions." He was in the air again, hissing and growling.

"*My name is Chloe!*" She matched his anger.

They stood glaring at each other across the hall. The anger ebbed away as Kerlvin's brows knitted and furrowed. He frowned at the look on Chloe's face. Her transparent eyes were huge. Heart starting to race, Kerlvin turned to see what she was staring at.

Black smoke was billowing from under the door at the end of the hall. Chloe could feel the hatred and sorrow seeping through the air. The hall was cold, the air heavy with pain. Chloe was backing slowly into the wall. Through the swirling black, Edgar's face appeared. His eyes locked onto Chloe's; she could feel the hate burning through them.

"Why won't you leave me alone?" he bellowed. The black mass flew toward her; Chloe squeaked, throwing her arms over her face. Nothing happened. Slowly she opened an eye. The swirling cloud was held fast, billowing and storming as if behind glass.

With a snap of his fingers, Kerlvin hissed, "Away, my pet; I am talking with the dead girl."

"Chloe," she muttered.

Ignoring her words, he explained without her asking. "I am here to watch over Edgar. My master charged me with keeping him here and safe," Kerlvin explained. "It is all very boring. We can't leave this house. I am away from my realm." The demon continued talking more to himself than to Chloe. "My claws don't tear; my teeth don't rend; my eyes do not bring fear. I miss the screams; I miss the pain. I miss my home."

"Is there something I can do to help you get home?" Chloe asked. Kerlvin jumped as if he forgot she was there.

Scratching a claw on the scruff of black hair on his chin, he appraised her. "Only the one who holds the tokens can release me," Kerlvin grumbled nodding. "If the tokens were found and returned to the dead, then I can collect the guilty and take them to my castle in hell." He saw the look on her face. "Oh, yes, I may be a lesser demon, but I still have a castle; my clan has held the lands of the blood hills for millennia."

"Oh, um, is it nice there?"

"The hills run with blood; the screams of the damned howl throughout the endless storm of burning rain. The land squelches underfoot as it is made of organs ripped from the bodies of captives. They feel each claw as it cuts and scratches, each tooth as it tears and eats. The air is filled with the smell of rot, vile, and putrefaction," he explained.

"Oh...I'm uh..." Chloe began.

"It is glorious." Kerlvin interrupted, a look of pure bliss on his face.

"Riight, so where can I find the tokens?"

"I can't tell you." He shrugged. "Don't know." With a snap of his fingers, Edgar evaporated back under the door. Kerlvin rose in the air under the heavy beat of his leathery wings. Flying up through a crack in the ceiling, he glanced back. "I will keep Edgar confined while you look, you and your human friends," he called, disappearing into the dark.

THE CONSERVATORY

Searching as they went, Alex followed Aaron to the front door. "Dude, I'm sorry. I don't know where she went," Alex pleaded. Aaron waved him off irritably. With one hand on the doorknob, Aaron turned to tell his younger brother off. Alex waited, but Aaron didn't move or speak, his mouth still starting to form the first words of a tirade. Alex stared at his brother. Aaron's gaze went past Alex's head toward the stairs. Alex slowly turned. Cold dread filled his stomach as he dared to look at what had distracted Aaron.

Alex's legs turned to jelly as relief washed over him. "Chloe, what happened? Where did you go?"

She was also looking past Alex. "Is he OK?"

"Yeah, he's just a dork," Alex assured.

"Dork?" she asked as she approached, slowly descending the stairs. Alex's eyes rolled along with a slight shake of his head when he heard the unmistakable sound of Aaron backing into the closed front door. Chloe stuttered to a stop, slightly backing away. Aaron's eyes were the size of dinner plates. Cold fear enveloped her. She was ready to disappear. "What is it?" she cried back up close to Alex. Aaron whimpered. Behind her was nothing except an empty stair. "Oh..." She realized, floating forward, head down in embarrassment. "It's me." She turned to face them.

The sadness crossing her face tugged at Alex's heart. "Damn it, Aaron," he exclaimed, punching his brother in the shoulder. "That's Chloe. She's great. Now stop being a douche." He turned to face her. "I was worried when I couldn't find you."

"Can we return to the conservatory? There is something I need to tell you," she asked, a slight pink showing through her pallor. Alex followed down the hall. She turned but continued to float backward. "I'm great?" she whispered through a smile as he followed. Aaron made a noise somewhere between a whimper and a gag. Alex had turned to inspect a painting. He was oblivious to Chloe's statement. He turned to his brother questioningly.

"Just keep going." Aaron waved, trepidation etched on his face as he watched the specter lead the way. Reaching the safety of her conservatory, Chloe explained what had happened. As Alex questioned if Chloe was OK, Aaron sank to the floor.

"Too much, man—too much," he muttered. "I mean, shit, it is bad enough the house is haunted...no offense." He nodded to Chloe.

"None taken," she replied.

He continued as if he hadn't even heard her. "Now I hear we have a demon and some kind of über-angry killer ghost!" Aaron was back on his feet. "I mean, fantastic! What the hell are we gonna tell Dad?"

"Kerlvin assured me he would keep Edgar in the back bedroom—" Chloe began.

"Oh, well, that's fine then. I feel so much better the demon made assurances!" Aaron shouted.

Alex jumped between his brother and the rapidly vanishing Chloe. "Whoa, whoa! Chill out, man! Chloe, don't go, please. Aaron, relax!" Alex began to pace. Chloe had become more visible, but her eyes told him she was a breath away from leaving. Aaron, on the other hand, was breathing like an angry bull. "OK, first things first." Alex inhaled. "Aaron, apologize to Chloe."

Aaron looked like he'd been slapped. Chloe immediately came to his defense. "No, he is right." She sighed. "I am trusting a demon to keep a murdering spirit at bay." The silence stretched on.

"Right, well, it is better than nothing, I guess..." Aaron conceded feebly.

"OK, um...great," Alex replied. He thought for a moment, aware that the others were watching him. "Let's take this Kerlvin at his word and assume we can get some work done." Alex chewed his bottom lip. "And while we do that, we look for these tokens. I think the demon will keep his end of things if he thinks it will get him home."

"If he isn't lying," Aaron muttered.

"I might finally get to leave as well," Chloe replied. The effect was not what any of them expected. Alex found his excitement to find the tokens immediately calmed. Aaron looked torn, while Chloe seemed confused.

"Well, great, then," Aaron said, rubbing the back of his neck. "I'll tell Dad we can start to work soon." His hands fell to his sides; he shrugged. "Yeah, let's do that." Aaron turned, making his way out of the conservatory. Moments later, they heard the echo of the front door shutting.

Alex faced Chloe. Smiling, he placed his hands as best as he could on her upper arms. "Thanks for helping us out. I really appreciate it." Letting his hands fall, he could not meet her eyes as he said, "And if you would like"—he swallowed nervously—"we can um move your...body to a...I mean, give you a proper buri..."

She was quickly waving away his statement before he could finish. "We found my earring here. Maybe..." She closed her eyes in concentration, thinking hard. "Maybe..." She paused. "Since this is the newest part of the house, they would be here.

You know, the tokens or whatever." She was already turning, looking around like it would be in a box sitting in the middle of the floor.

Alex reached out, touching her hand. "According to Dad, there was another addition added in the forties and several renovations." She turned to face him. The pale blue of her eyes stared into his heart. Looking away, he replied, "I just don't want you to get your hopes up too much." Again he couldn't face her. "I mean, it is possible they have already been discovered and thrown out." He felt a pressure on his arm. Turning back, he was struck by the infectious enthusiastic smile on her face.

"If that were true..." She laughed. "Then there would be no need for a little demon to be hanging around, would there?" Smiling as well, he agreed, spending the next several hours clearing out old flowerbeds and dirty alcoves. As Alex pulled out weeds and plants, Chloe dove through the dirt and into the walls. Several families of insects and rodents were disturbed, but little else was found.

1952

Edgar lay on the filthy, stained mattress listening to the birds of early spring call for mates. He didn't really lie as much as float above the dingy mold. The songs of the birds along with the bright, warm light filtering through the dust annoyed him. Rising, he decided to wander through the empty house. Since his death, he had been so bored. The little demon had seemed to lose interest in him after the first couple of years. Now he would welcome the torment the creature gave him as a remedy to his boredom.

This was the punishment for his sins, he decided. He accepted he was in his own personal hell. Gliding through the door, he was out in the hall. The paper was starting to peel, and dust lay thick on all the surfaces. A frown creased his face. Something had been chewing on the once-elegant carpet of the hall. "Why didn't that retched Kerlvin chase it away?" he muttered. Gliding farther down the hall, he got the answer. A huge rat lay at the top of the stairs, its innards strewn and smeared over the topmost step. From the color and stench, it had been there awhile. There were signs Kerlvin had "played" with the rat prior to its demise. Edgar's observations were interrupted by the opening of the front door.

A shadow passed across the light then was immediately cut off by the slamming of the front door. Edgar found his curiosity piqued. The door had not been forced. Maybe it was his brother coming to visit finally. If Edgar could make Richard see him, maybe he wouldn't be alone anymore. Richard had promised to take care of him. Richard would visit him. He would figure out a way to free him from the house.

Gliding quickly down the stairs, he was on the ground floor in seconds. Looking left and right, he tried to find whoever had entered. Something moved in the front room. Edgar was at the threshold about to enter when sharp claws dug into his shoulder. Edgar fought to free himself. He could see a cloaked figure crouching in the room. A scraping of metal on wood emanated from the room. Someone was trying to rob him, and this wretched demon was keeping him from defending his property.

Edgar pulled free of the claws. He was about to enter the room. His anger flared. He could feel his eyes burn, his vision clouded in red. Pain seared through his neck. Kerlvin cackled. His wings beat hard, pulling Edgar out of the room. He flailed, trying to hit the demon. His anger and frustration only grew as his hands simply went through the black scaly body. He swung again, crying out in pain when Kerlvin sunk his razor-sharp teeth into Edgar's hand.

"How can you hurt me when I can't even touch you?" Edgar thundered. His answer was a cackle from Kerlvin. "I'm being robbed! Let me go!" Edgar pleaded.

The cloaked figure was back in the hall. He took no notice of the ghost and the demon fighting a few feet away. Edgar was being pulled up toward the ceiling. The talons ripped through his flesh. He could feel the burning pain. Edgar was shocked at the flow of sticky blood and the cold of the air on the open wound. Before he hit the ground, he felt knives digging into his shoulders. Deeply, Kerlvin's talons pierced his flesh. Edgar could feel them grasp onto bone. He was flung up in the air, spun, and was caught. The demon's claws ripped through flesh again and were now holding him by his rib cage. He thrashed, trying to rip out Kerlvin's eyes. The demon no longer cackled. Venom-soaked words spat from his forked black tongue. "You will be punished for fighting me." Edgar screamed in agony. The bones of his rib cage shattered as they were torn from his chest. The front door slammed at the same time Edgar smashed to the floor. Kerlvin was on him in a flash, ripping at his flesh, pulling organs free. Blood sprayed over the walls.

"How?...How?...I'm already...dead." Edgar gasped as his arm was torn free.

"I have power over you. I can destroy you again." Kerlvin punctuated this by pulling intestine from Edgar's gut. "And again." He flung out the liver. "And again." Edgar's stomach, bloated and pink, slapped against the wall. "And you will feel every cut." Kerlvin slashed Edgar's face. "Every bruise." He punched him hard. "For eternity. You will never feel peace, you will never defend this house's possessions, and you will never be the king of this castle." Kerlvin pulled Edgar's head from his body. Edgar's eyes, wide with surprise, were held close to the demon's face; the last thing his ears heard was, "I am."

With a cry, Edgar awoke on the filthy bed. He ran his hands over his body. It was all there, all intact and all transparent and as substantial as smoke. A snicker at the foot of the bed poured ice through his spine.

"Learned a valuable lesson, did we?"

Edgar raised his head enough to see the demon crouched on the footboard. Slowly Kerlvin extended his wings and was gone. Edgar's vision blurred red with hatred; his hands became less defined as a black shimmer of anger surrounded him.

HOUSE WORK

The front room was unrecognizable. The walls were clean and repaired, the floors sanded and stained. The ancient rug and furniture completely cleaned and restored. A beautiful new light hung from the ceiling with brand-new outlets and switches throughout. The work went fast with three men working and a fourth helper always around. Alex's father took the longest to get used to be observed by the pale gray girl in the long coat. She would spend most of her time in Alex's company. Arthur would hear them talking about the years following her death. "Well, Dad says the celebrations in 1976 for the bicentennial were amazing," Alex was explaining as Arthur entered the hall. Looking left and right, he could not see whom Alex was talking to. His heart jumped as her face appeared out of the wall to the young man's left.

"The wood looks rather eaten here," she explained as Alex walked over to make a mark under the smiling face. "Oh, hi, Arthur."

"Chloe." He nodded. "I was wondering if I could have a word with my son."

Chloe materialized through the wall, a quizzical look on her face. If she had a question, she did not ask. Alex watched her disappear down the hall before looking questioningly at his father. "Alex, I don't think this is fair," Arthur began. "Chloe is a great help, but..." He rubbed the back of his neck as he searched for what to say. "She doesn't belong here."

"Dad, she has more of a claim to this house than we do," Alex argued.

His father raised a hand to cut him off. "That is not what I am saying. I mean here in this existence." He blew out a breath. "We need to find a way to let her...pass on."

"But that is what we are trying to do." Alex then went on to explain about the meeting with Kerlvin and the tokens. Arthur was horrified at the thought of a demon holding back a being of pure anger in the back bedroom as they restored the house. Alex explained that the finding of the tokens would send all of them on their way. He explained what happened when he returned the earring.

"What about the shoe you found in Granddad's old stuff?" Arthur asked.

Slapping himself in the forehead, he said, "Holy shit! I forgot all about that." Alex exclaimed, then apologized to his father for the language. Arthur laughed with a shake of his head.

Before he could tell his son that at age nineteen he was allowed to swear, Aaron burst through the front door. "There's another one!" he cried. Doubled over, gasping for breath, he held out a hand telling them he had more to say. Chloe appeared in the hall, causing Aaron to shriek. Hand on his heart, he fell against the wall. "Oh, it's only you." Chloe's face crumpled into irritation. "Listen, sorry," Aaron spoke, still trying to get his breathing under control. "I was out back. You know, inspecting the fence and noting the property line." Alex disappeared into the next room, returning with a bottled of water. Aaron took the drink, finishing it in a couple of seconds. He looked up at the expectant eyes. "Right, well, I was by these trees when I heard a voice. At first I thought it was you." He pointed at Chloe. "But then I saw her. Her hair was shorter, and I could see..." He swallowed, closing his eyes tight as if trying to rid them of the vision. "She had been shot, at least twice. Once in the chest." He pointed to his own, close to his neck. "You could see the stain on her bare skin and the wound." He tipped the empty bottle up; a single drop hit his tongue. Chloe swooped out of the room. Quickly she returned with another bottle, handing it over. "Thanks." He took a couple of gulps. "I could see the hole in her head. When she saw me, she started screaming at me, calling me a murderer." Aaron took a deep breath. "I tried to tell her it wasn't me..." A strange look crossed Aaron's face. "How did you do that?" He was staring at Chloe.

"I didn't kill her," she sputtered.

Aaron was now looking at the bottle in his hand. "No, I mean this." He held it out to her. She stared at it, confused. She looked at the others and saw they were also staring at the clear plastic vessel. She reached out. Her hand passed right through the bottle. Frowning, she tried again.

"I don't know." She sighed. Chloe concentrated. She had done this once before when she knocked over the bust in the conservatory. "Give me a second." She tried again, and again her hand passed right through. Frustrated, she tried once more. Aaron's hand moved when Chloe's contacted the bottle. She took it from him, marveling at in her grasp. She cried out in a whoop of joy.

Congratulating Chloe, Alex then asked the question on everyone's mind. "Do you know who this other girl is?" The bottle hit the floor with an empty thud. Chloe's attention was now on Alex.

"I don't know. I haven't left this house in something like eighty years. I have no idea how long I was alone at the bottom of the well."

"Well?" Arthur asked.

"Yeah, Chloe's body is in a well under the floor in the conservatory," Alex explained as if this was common knowledge.

He ignored his father's sputtering. "We need to figure out who she was."

"And how many others are out there." Chloe agreed.

Aaron and Arthur watched the interaction, Alex turned to the door. He grabbed Chloe's hand. Instantly she was shocked by the feeling. At the door she pulled free. "I can't, remember?" She stared past him out through the opening.

"Right, sorry." He touched her face gently. "Aaron, come on, I want to meet your new girlfriend." Aaron looked stricken. Arthur began to protest. "We need to find out who she is and what she is missing."

"I'd say the back of her head and any patience for me," Aaron protested.

"Dude, I need you to show me where she is," Alex explained. Looking over at the frightened look Chloe wore, he stepped in front of her, blocking the view of the porch and lawn. "Chloe, can you stay here and help Dad with some of the wiring?" She nodded, moving closer to Arthur.

"I don't want you boys doing anything foolish. She lashes out, you run. You got that?" Arthur ordered. The boys had passed out the door when Chloe called after them.

"That is sound advice. If she is like me, she will be trapped in one place." She couldn't see the pained look on Alex's face. "If she turns out to be like Edgar, run, just run. He is pure anger now."

The sun was already making its descent below the trees when the two men stepped off the porch and took the turn toward the woods. "Maybe this should wait until tomorrow," Aaron whispered. Alex shushed him.

1938

Edgar's breath hung in the icy air. He shivered as he made his way deeper into the old barn. He puzzled as the outside air had been so warm on this late July evening. There was a light in the back and muffled voices. Edgar was rooted to the ground, his heart hammering away. *As if this night needed to get worse*, he thought. He had just left the main house after yet another heated discussion with his father.

"You are a disappointment to me and a disgrace to the family," his father had growled during dinner. Edgar had just lost one of the mill's oldest clients due to missing several deadlines. "I don't know why I ever thought putting you in charge would change you," the elder man continued as Edgar twisted his napkin in his lap. Richard stared at his brother, shaking his head slightly, warning Edgar not to react. "If your brother wasn't so busy with his studies, I would have him take over at once." Mr. Davis's hand slammed the table, sending the glasses tinkling and silverware clinking.

"Father," Richard began. "I would not want that job. It is thankless." He sighed heavily. "The clients have unrealistic expectations. I believe their problem is more with Edgar trying to run the business effectively than any fault of his own. Under the previous management, they were given too—"

"If it is not his fault, he can answer for himself!" The elder Davis slammed his hand down again.

Both Edgar and Richard sat in stunned silence. Their father never raised his voice to his young son. Their mother smiled as if oblivious to the raised voices and murderous looks. "I think a little sip would do us all good." She got unsteadily to her feet, bustling over to a cabinet in the corner. "I don't really care what the president says; a little nip never hurt anyone." She made to pour some amber liquid in Mr. Davis's glass, but he covered it with his hand.

"I believe it was a little nip that caused most of our troubles at the mill. Perhaps not so little." Mr. Davis was glaring at his eldest son. Edgar took the glass his mother had just filled for him and downed it in one go.

"Attaboy," his mother cried as she downed her own drink. Richard stared at his own untouched glass. He watched as his brother's drink was refilled by their mother. He knew where this evening was going and excused himself. His mother shrugged, taking his drink and finished it before he was out of the room.

Disgust crumpled Mr. Davis's face. "You both are repulsive. Stay here with your mother, boy. When you grow to be a man, come back to talk to me."

Mrs. Davis laughed at her husband's back while she poured two more drinks. "When you can prove to me you're a man, maybe I'll let him go." Her glare could burn through steel. Mr. Davis half-turned back to the room. Edgar's drink shook in his hand as he waited for the verbal tornado to fall. It didn't. His father left the room to the cackle of laughter of his mother. Edgar had sat drinking with her until the second bottle was half-empty, and she got up to continue the fight with Mr. Davis. Edgar left the house to angry screams of his mother calling for his father and the shattering of glass.

A board creaked under Edgar's boot. In an instant the barn was silent and dark. The air began to warm. A silhouette appeared as the back door was thrown open and disappeared with the slamming door. Edgar listened for a moment, making sure he was alone. Another fear jabbed into his stomach. *What if they knew? What if they found his secret?* Quickly lighting a lamp, he rushed behind the bales and discarded timber. Straw was strewn over the floor, covering charred wood. Brushing off the board with the knot in it, he disregarded the symbols carved into it. *More of Richard's doodles,* he thought. Throwing the board aside, relief washed over him. It was still there; he was still safe.

Edgar woke the next morning with a band saw ripping through his skull and cats fighting in his stomach. Dangerously, he got to his feet. Bending over to replace the board and cover it with straw nearly killed him, or so it felt. Stumbling out in the blazing sun, he threw up. Today was not going to be a good day. His father was on the porch now. Edgar waited for the berating. None came. His father stared at him, blood appeared on his mouth, and the older man fell.

At the hospital, the doctors couldn't tell the family what was wrong, but it didn't look good. Edgar wasn't sure how he felt, but there was something odd about his brother's blank stare. He couldn't tell if he was satisfied or terrified.

THE BACK FORTY

"How much farther?" Alex asked. At first Aaron did not answer.

"Don't you think it is getting too dark?"

"Come on; we need get moving."

"Listen, man, you don't get it," Aaron hissed. "This one isn't like your girlfriend back at the house."

Alex stopped dead; Aaron ran into him with an "oomph."

"Chloe is not my girlfriend."

"Yeah, 'cause she is dead." Aaron snickered. "'Bout the only way you could get a girl to put up with you."

Alex's retort was drowned out by the mournful cry filling the air. The sound was all around and in them. The weight of sadness it held settled in his chest. A tear ran down his cheek; his heart swirled in a whirlpool of despair. His shoulders slumped under the burden of crippling depression.

"Alex, you OK?" Aaron's hand was on his brother's shoulder. "Come on, man; what's the matter?" Alex saw the fear in his brother's eyes, but all he could do is shudder as a sob racked his body.

"Murder," called a mournful cried carried on the wind. "You left me here." Alex stumbled forward, blinded by tears. Aaron pulled on Alex's arm to no avail, trying to return to the house. "All I wanted was to go home. Why wouldn't you let me go home?" She continued to wail.

Alex pushed through the low-hanging branches into the darkness of a small clearing, Aaron muttering at his side, "We can't even see the house. Dad won't be able to help us." Alex was oblivious to the protests.

"I want to go *home*!" Leaves burst into the air in an icy blast. Branches and twigs scratched their faces and outstretched hands. An old bottle flew past Aaron's ear. He followed its flight.

"Edgar," he muttered.

"Murderer!" an apparition shouted. She stood in the clearing pointing an accusing finger at Aaron. Her face was gaunt with deep dark-set eyes. The blood stains reflected silvery in the emerging moonlight.

"Please," Alex whispered. The ghost turned slowly. She stared as if just noticing Alex. "Please, we want to help," he choked out through his tears.

"Help? Help! *Help!*" the figure screamed, volume increasing with each word. Aaron pulled Alex back. The wind was swirling around the pale form in the center of the clearing. "I screamed for help! I begged for help! No one came!" The two men ducked behind a fallen tree. The wind became a roar, yet they could still hear every word the apparition spoke, her frantic anger matching the howling wind. "I never sleep; I never eat; I never get tired; I...just...*am!*" she screamed. The crash of a large branch rocked the log they hid behind.

"That wasn't us," Alex shouted. "We just want to help."

"All I wanted to do was go home. I worked at the diner. Every Tuesday that drunken bastard would come in to bother me. I told him I had a boyfriend. I told him I was true." Several rocks flew past their heads. "He killed me! I woke in this clearing cold and scared. My head hurt." The wind began to die down. "I was leaving work. There was someone behind me. I knew it was Edgar, and then I woke up here." She was pointing to something brownish white uncovered by the blowing and swirling wind. "I could see his silhouette from the moon." She was gazing up at the sky. Alex and Aaron dared to look as the wind was barely a breeze. "I heard the gun and felt a burning in my chest, then in my head." She looked over at the place where a bone was visible on the ground. "I fell," she whispered. With a wave of her hand, the remaining leaves and dirt flew away, revealing most of a skeleton. "I'm still here! Days have passed, years, and no one came to find me." Her attention was fully back on the pale faces of the two men barely visible over the rotting log. When she started speaking, her voice was quiet and calm. "He buried me." The air became deadly calm except for the frantic whispers of Aaron attempting to get Alex to run. An angry blast of icy wind and white-blue flame erupted around her. "I'm still here!" She screamed, "Why am I still *here!*"

Aaron gave up on his brother and broke for the house. Alex slowly stood up to face her. Skeletal in appearance now, she resembled more the thing in the grave than the woman who had appeared first. The eyes were black holes surrounded by loose-hanging skin. Her teeth were exposed; the hole in her head was seeping something black and putrid. "Animals took my hands and feet; they ate my eyes; I could feel the insects eating me." The ground became scorched around her as wave after wave of burning cold pulsed outward. "I felt it all."

"What did he take?" Alex called in a last effort to avoid her wrath.

"*He took my life!*" The wall of ice fire slammed Alex to the ground. Every exposed area felt the burn of biting cold. "I was cold, so cold. Cold is all I ever feel." She threw another wall of ice at him. Her hands stayed spread in front of her. The wind and the cold died away. Alex tried to catch his breath, tried to inhale any warmth he could. "My ring," she stated simply. "It was two small pearls: one white, one gray. When I died, he pulled it off my finger. It was gone before the fox took my hand." She was hovering over Alex now, her face a mask of confusion. "I died for my ring?"

Alex scuttled away from her. "You died so he could live. He made a deal with the devil. He needed your ring to...to..." He could see the anger beginning to creep back into her features. "I think bind your energy to him."

Silence met this statement. Her head was cocked to one side, a look of dawning spreading across her features. "His grandmother *was* a witch." She began to take on a more human appearance again. Alex slowly got to his feet; holding his hands up, he stepped tentatively over the log. She was muttering something as he approached. Alex could only make out the words *killer* and *dead*. He was very close to her now. He could see the detail of the holes in her body, the dirt covering her clothing and the name embroidered on the dress, "Brenda."

"Brenda?" Alex whispered. The reaction was immediate.

"Yes? Do I know you?" Brenda asked. She smiled at him; it was a kind smile.

"Your name is Brenda, Brenda what?" he asked holding out his hand.

"Brenda Rhodes, and you are?" She held out her own hand, and the air froze. She was staring at their hands, almost touching. Alex closed his eyes, shaking his head slightly as he realized his mistake. "Murderer!" she screamed as the wind rose. Heavy hands slammed down on Alex's shoulders, yanking him backward. Alex could hear his father screaming at Brenda from the other side of the clearing. Ducking low, avoiding the flying debris, Alex and Aaron ran for the house. They could hear their father crashing after them.

CONSEQUENCES

Out of sight of Brenda, the howling wind died down. Alex's hands were on his knees as he struggled to regain his breath. Aaron leaned against a tree, wheezing, while their father paced angrily. "What the hell was that all about?" he demanded.

Before Alex could answer, Aaron's startled cry called their attention to him. The sight ahead caused Aaron and Arthur to recoil in terror. For Alex, the sight ripped through his heart. Chloe struggled toward him. The pull of the house caused every step to be a war. With each inch she strayed, another piece was torn from her. Ragged shattered bone stuck out from the shredded coat sleeve. She fell when her leg and hip exploded. Her face was a tight mask pulled over the skull. Alex flew to her side. Her skeletal broken fingers clawed at the ground.

"You're safe." A harsh rasping voice rattled from the desiccated throat. Her smile split the skin at the corners of her mouth.

"What is happening to her?" Aaron cried over Alex's shoulder.

Arthur was there now. "She's too far from the house. We have to get her back there."

It felt like sliding his hands under a bundle of broken sticks. His tears fell as did pieces of bones, raining in a ghostly glow onto the ground. Chloe moaned in agony as Alex lifted her. She weighed nothing in his arms. Alex tried to run. Chloe's cries kept him to a tentative pace. There was an assault on their ears with every step. Bones snapped and shattered and reformed. Chloe screamed, and dark silvery blood oozed back into gaping wounds. Alex stumbled blindly, tears obscuring his sight. Alex could hear his father speaking soft words to Chloe as he walked by their side, stroking at first skull, then hair. Aaron led the group slowly back to the house through the darkness. The warmth of his hand felt comforting on Alex's arm.

The hollow thud of Alex's shoe on the wooden porch was easily heard through the deadly silence. Chloe had become heavier with every step, but she also became quieter. Alex had not dared to look down until they reached the hall. Laying her carefully on a chaise in the front room, Alex collapsed in a heap next to her. Arthur's hand gripped Alex's shoulder. "She's back now; she'll be OK."

Aaron gasped, "We lost a shoe!" He was pointing at Chloe's feet. Alex stared, his mind clouded and slow. She was indeed missing a shoe.

Arthur was in action now. There was quick movement behind Alex as he continued to stare. The outline of her toes through the sock was familiar. He had noticed it often since they met. They could not have lost it. Flashlights were tested, and a lantern dazzled Alex back to reality.

"Wait! We didn't lose her shoe. She didn't have one on..." Alex slapped himself in the head. Quickly he whispered in Arthur's ear. Arthur stood up straight, glaring down at his son. He gave Alex a soft slap to the back of the head and hurried out the door, the truck keys jingling. Aaron watched his father go. A clicking sound from the corner began to annoy Aaron.

"Where did Dad go, and what the hell is that clicking?" Aaron turned to see Kerlvin tapping a clawed toe on the bottom stair. A cry of terror found Aaron scuttling back to his brother. He pointed, mouth open, at the demon.

"Tell her that was very foolish," the demon hissed. His wings unfurled, and he took flight. "Tell her she has to be here, or there is no way for either of us to be free." He disappeared in a flurry of wings and dust.

"What the hell is going *on*!" Aaron shouted. Several long minutes later had Alex still sitting next to Chloe holding her hand; she had not stirred. Aaron paced angrily up and down the hall. Frustrated, he stopped behind his brother. "She's a ghost." It was not a question. "But you can carry her! You can hold her hand; you, you...I mean, what the hell?" He ran a hand through Chloe. Alex jumped up glaring at Aaron. "See I can't touch her, but you." He pointed accusingly at Alex.

"You think I know? You think I care?" Alex growled. "She needed me, and I was there that is all that matters." Aaron backed away. His brother's ferocity surprised him. "I can't let anything happen to her. Like that runty demon says, she needs to be here so we can let her rest." A tear ran down Alex's cheek.

"Al, she's dead." Aaron's voice was soft. "You can't...." The front door swung open. Arthur held out an old box.

"I can't believe you forgot about this. Again!" He frowned at Alex.

"Sorry," Alex muttered, but Aaron wasn't sure who he was apologizing to. From the box he pulled an old small shoe. Slowly he knelt down next to Chloe's still figure. Alex carefully lifted the shoeless foot. Arthur's arm rested on Aaron's shoulder. Alex slipped the shoe over Chloe's toes, adjusting the strap. Aaron gasped. Chloe was more substantial. Her eyes cracked open. She inhaled. With the breath she seemed to also inhale color and substance. The chaise was still visible beneath her but much less so.

"I begged my father for those." She spoke weakly as he slowly sat up. Alex's arm was behind her helping her up. "He told me we couldn't afford them." She smiled, holding her feet out in front to get a better look. "Then he came home one day with the box. He said they went well with the coat." Tears slid down her cheeks. "He said a proper young lady needed good shoes." Her smile was sad as she let her feet drop to the floor. Her hand caressed Alex's face.

"My father found that." Arthur spoke: "I'm sorry it took us so long to get it back to you."

"Your father was always so wonderful. I miss him," Chloe replied.

"So do I."

"I still have no idea what the hell is going on!" Aaron huffed.

RESEARCH

After the events in the woods, it took a couple of days and the combined arguments of Chloe and Albert to get Alex to leave Chloe and the house. It was a question posed by Aaron that finally got Alex motivated. "How many more girls did Edgar kill?" The silence that followed was deafening. Alex looked over at Chloe and decided to make it his mission to find out.

Chloe remembered Brenda from the diner. Although other than remembering she was always very nice, there was nothing more she could tell him. Alex began spending less time helping with the restoration and more time at the library and local historical society. He would return every evening to do a few things, but mostly he spent his time talking with Chloe to the annoyance of his brother. He never said anything because of the look he got from Arthur whenever he started to complain.

More and more often, Alex would return to find Chloe with his father. Sometimes they would have their heads together working on the electric; sometimes they would argue over the HVAC. Sometimes it was just quiet conversation about Alex's grandfather as a youth.

"I miss working with my father on the tractors. This feels good," Chloe had explained.

"On top of that, I don't need to rip out the walls to get things done. Our girl"—Albert waved at Chloe, who blushed at the statement—"can really get into those hard-to-reach places." Alex knew she was still trying to find the missing items taken from her and however many others were out there. The thought of more people trapped in the places they died gnawed at him at night.

Aaron still wasn't as eager to work with Chloe. They were very courteous with each other. Aaron remained rather standoffish. They chatted occasionally while he worked, but mostly he stayed distant. Chloe shrugged at his coolness as if it didn't bother her, but Alex could tell it did. She stated she liked Aaron but had no idea how to talk to him. When Alex asked Aaron why he rarely interacted with her, Aaron explained, "I just don't want to get too attached." He gave Alex a pointed look that Alex brushed off, but the feeling in the pit of his stomach only grew.

A new day found Alex back in the library. He had already been through the newspapers that covered Chloe's disappearance. It annoyed him how little enthusiasm the reporter had for the story. The reports angered Alex. There was never any mention of the police interview with Edgar. It took hours and hours of combing through the columns for Alex to even find Brenda's name. She had disappeared six months after Chloe. He found another name in a paper six months after the mention of Brenda. The young woman was Gay Cleary. It was then that Alex noticed the date. It was the one-year anniversary of when Chloe had gone missing.

Going back in his research, he found the date of Brenda's disappearance. It was exactly six months after Chloe's. Excited but dreading what he might find, he checked ahead another six months. There was nothing. At the two-year anniversary, another girl went missing. Oddly, at years three and four, there was no mention of any missing girls. At the five-year anniversary, he found a small article about another girl gone missing. The disappearances were getting further apart. Alex tried to do the math, coming to the conclusion that there had been thirteen deaths so far, and the day for the next murder was fast approaching. That was if Edgar had lived. With a note of anger, Alex noted more column space was devoted years later to the death of the elder Mr. Davis and passing of the family business to Edgar than to any of the missing women.

It was weird, though. It didn't look like Edgar was keeping his end of whatever bargain he had made. There was trouble at the mill, layoffs, union troubles, and safety violations. This is when he found Edgar's name in prominence. It was always connected to some scandal or bad business dealings. After 1947, Alex couldn't find any more missing-persons reports. After weeks of research, he decided he had found out all he could from the old papers.

Next was the county courthouse. The land deeds and tax records told little, but a clerk he met turned out to be the curator of the county historical society. Here, Alex was told many interesting stories. This was the source of information he needed, he thought.

Storied Past

"Oh so you are the ones who are brave enough to buy the old Sterben place," Beverly Grasso asked, a sly grin spreading across her face. "Makes sense once you learn the history." She gave him an appraising look. "Which I really doubt you know." Alex wasn't sure he liked this woman, who had been in charge of the county historical society for more than thirty years. Looking over the dusty displays and ancient books Alex thought this was because no one else wanted or cared about the job. Beverly, however, clearly did not share this view. A quick look around the room showed she seemed to focus most of the society's research on the Sterben house. "The history of that house is extremely interesting, intriguing, and,"—she dropped her voice to conspiratorial whisper—"evil." She then back away, looking him carefully up and down. Alex felt like he was being X-rayed. He waited. He tried to continue smiling benignly at the older woman. Suddenly she seemed to come to a conclusion. Slapping the desk causing Alex to jump, she motioned to a chair as she sat heavily on an old leather high-back one behind the desk. "Well, the original owners, the Von Sterbens, who I believe your grandmother was a descendant of..."

"Um, sure, if you say so. Grandad said we had a connection to the house, but it had been out of the family for years," Alex replied with a shrug. "Some kind of scandal that hurt a lot of people." A dark cloud covered his face. "Something that people are still asses about. Sorry," he grumbled about his language.

Continuing on as if she hadn't heard anything, she said, "Well, they had been a well-liked and respected family in the area, founding members of the community, very civic-minded."

Beverly sighed. "But due to that scandalous misfortune, along with strange sickness and early deaths, the family fell on hard times." She searched through some papers. Pulling out an old newspaper that Alex hadn't seen in the archives, she waved it in his face. "It was quite salacious."

The headline read *Prominent Man Guilty of Inappropriate Conduct*. Alex snatched the paper from her. His eyes burned through the information. It spoke of prostitutes, larceny, and underhanded dealings with the underworld. The thing that struck him like a punch in the stomach was the word *murder*. Scanning farther, Alex's eyes bulged at the information. His ancestor was being accused of setting the fire that had killed Edgar's grandmother.

"What happened with the murder charge?" Alex croaked; his throat was a desert. He looked up to see Beverly watching him closely.

"Hmm, I see not something the family discussed often, eh?" She laughed. It was more of a rasping cackle. "Charges were never filed. Never enough evidence." Leaning forward and lowering her voice, she said, "It didn't matter, though. The rumors ruined him. None of the things the family was accused of stuck." Her tone dropped lower. "It didn't matter. They were ruined, and then the Davis family began to prosper." She leaned back slowly. "When your family was forced to sell off the house and business, public opinion was that they should just give the Davis's the keys and leave town."

"Well, my family didn't do that, now did we?" Alex frowned. "Would have been better if we had," he muttered.

Ignoring him, Beverly was rummaging through the papers on her desk. With a flourish, she found what she was looking for. An old photo was thrust into Alex's hands. It showed several people standing in front of a much smaller version of

the house where Chloe was. "This was from a better time." She smiled slightly. "The house was eventually sold to the Davis family." Beverly continued without letting Alex spend too much time with the old photo. She was rummaging again. "Well, the Davis's were not nearly as well liked." An old box top was flung over, dust flying into the air. "It was later rumored that Old Lady Davis was a witch." Another ancient photo was thrust in front of him. The woman pictured was hunched and decrepit-looking. Her eyes were the only thing in the picture in focus, and they burned with malice. The picture was snatched back. Beverly was happily back to digging in a box. "It was rumored she was behind the troubles with the Sterben family. Couldn't prove it, though, could they? Since she was dead." Alex opened his mouth, but the question was not allowed. "Oh, she was murdered all right, killed out in that shack in the woods." Her eyes filled with excitement as she told the tales. "Police eventually said it was an accidental fire. Bah!" She waved the idea away. "So the house gets bought by Old Man Davis, who brings his alcoholic wife and two boys to live there." Another photograph landed in front of Alex. His hand slammed down on it, holding it in place.

A cruel smile crossed Beverly's face. "Yes, that is Edgar," she said. Alex, surprised, met her gaze. "Evil man, that Edgar," she proclaimed, looking at the picture upside down. Her finger tapped the taller young man standing next to a severe-looking older man. Next to Edgar was a handsome man with an easy smile. The finger tapped next on this young face. "That is Richard. He tried to be a protector of Edgar, who was always in trouble with their father." She sighed. "Never had the brains, that Edgar. Then there are the rumors." She stared straight into his eyes. "You might know that they are not rumors. You are at the house. Have you seen it?" Alex thought she was referring to

Chloe. His mouth opened to protest, but he was cut off. "Not the girl," she interrupted as if she'd read his mind, "the dark mass of evil?"

Alex shivered. "Yes, I've seen him," he whispered.

"And her? Have you seen the girl?" Beverly had a manic look alight in her eyes.

"Yes," he hissed.

"Was it...was it...Brenda?" She demanded. "My great aunt went missing; was it Brenda?" She was standing right in front of him now.

"No," he stated, staring back into her gray eyes. She seemed to deflate. "But I met her."

"You...you met her? Where?"

Alex explained where Brenda was and his interaction with her. Beverly sat across from him and cried. "I always wanted to meet her. My mother spoke very highly of her. Maybe you could take me out there. You know, as a family member, I might be able to get through to her." Her eyes flew wide as she sprung to her feet.

"I am not sure that is the best idea," Alex explained uneasily. Beverly had started to scare him a little. He wondered if insanity ran in the family. "She was very angry, especially that no one came to find her. I think family might not calm her much." After a little back and forth, Beverly agreed to wait to meet Brenda. After that, she was all too happy to return to the history of Edgar and the house.

"After their father mysteriously died, the house passed to Edgar." It looked like Beverly had swallowed something horrid every time she spoke the name. "He lived there with his mother and Richard until she died, and Richard left to keep up and diversify the family business out in Pittsburgh." She returned to the boxes, pulling out a flyer calling for a strike at the mill. "Had to diversify as Edgar couldn't keep the mill profitable. This was just the beginning of the ugly business between the brothers," the clerk told Alex in hushed tones. "After Richard left, the two barely spoke again."

"What caused the quarrel?" Alex asked, thinking it likely involved money.

"Well, most people thought it was because of Edgar's gambling debts." Alex felt this had merit even though it was the first he'd heard of it. "I believe it was really about that girl who went missing right before my aunt did back in '32."

Alex sat up straight. "You mean Chloe Miller?"

"Yes, her." Beverly's manic look was back. "Richard never had a problem with the local girls; Edgar..."

"Not as handy with the ladies, I take it."

The clerk laughed, "Oh, no, no, no. He was never popular. I believe he was considered to be creepy. There were always stories about him trying to lure local girls into his car." Beverly sat back enjoying the effect this had on her audience. "Well, that young Miller girl had told her friends about an encounter the morning she went missing. Then she goes missing, and his truck has to get repaired? It was all very suspect, but the family had money, so the police couldn't fathom a boy of good breeding would do anything untoward." She snorted in disgust. "Didn't stop them ruining your family, did it?"

Alex frowned. "So, how does the brother come into play?" He realized he was literally on the edge of his seat.

"Edgar's story about a deer never sat well with many people. Richard spent a lot of time defending his brother. The thing is, too many things didn't add up. There was the damage to Edgar's truck, the fact that a well was demolished on the family property, something Edgar had been putting off for a while, and suddenly he gets it done without being asked. People were talking, and before you knew it, Richard left town. I guess he couldn't take the shame. I think he knew his brother did it."

"Why didn't he go to the police?"

"Couldn't prove anything, could he? No evidence against Edgar."

"So, what happened to Edgar? I know he died in the house." Alex leaned back in his chair.

"Oh, yes, killed there, he was. Gambling and drinking problem, that boy. Was always a drinker, but I think the guilt of the girls he killed—Chloe and my aunt aren't the only ones. We never thought he was smart enough to get away with it."

"So, who killed him?" Alex tried to get the conversation back on track.

Brenda took a moment to think. "Well, he was supposed to have dinner that night with a couple of the foremen from the mill." She rifled through a few papers, then held out a yellowing news clipping that was starting to turn to dust in his hands. "The one fellow, new in town, was killed, too. and the other guy went missing, so I think we know who did the other two in."

Alex read and reread the article. "Are you kidding me? Doesn't look like the police even bothered to investigate."

"After what he did? Did you really expect them to?" she countered. "By this point the town was just happy to be well rid of him." She patted his hand. "People in town had thought the first couple of girls had just run off, what with the Depression and all." She swiped at a tear. "But after the third girl went missing, then the fourth, people began to talk."

"Sorry," he mumbled. "I didn't mean to upset you. I just wanted justice for...for his victims."

"You just said what many here have felt for years." She shrugged. "Especially after the sightings started."

"Oh, you mean Chloe at the house, right?"

Beverly looked confused. "Chloe? You don't mean Chloe Miller, do you?" She shook her head slightly. "I've heard the rumors about the house." She stopped and stared at him. "Why would she be there?"

"Because that is where Edgar dumped her body, in the well?" he reminded her.

"Yes, but that is not where she died, surely."

"It was," Alex replied.

"Oh, how horrible; that means she was alive after he hit her." Beverly's hands covered her mouth, the horror written in her eyes.

"Yes, she was, but if you aren't talking about her, then who?"

Leaning forward, her voice dropped to a conspiratorial whisper: "Gay, Patricia Gay. She has been seen down at the lake for years. Usually when someone is in trouble, boating problem or tired from swimming, you'll see her rise out of the water and point to where trouble is. Never says a word, just points."

Alex sat for a moment. "Thank you for all of your help," he finally mumbled, lost in thought. Before he even opened the door to leave the building, he decided to head to the lake the next day.

AT THE LAKE

His stomach began to tie in knots as Alex slowed his car in the parking lot of the picnic area next to the lake. "It's huge," he grumbled to the steering wheel. "I can't believe this." Gravel crunched underfoot as he stepped clear of the car. The dull thud of the door sent a few birds scattering from the trees. It was late in the season, with most of the leaves already off the trees. The air was crisp and the rest of the lot empty.

"All right, sparky," he said to himself. "How are we going to get Ms. Gay's attention?" Walking the small bike path along the shore, Alex tried to think what Edgar would do. "He wasn't a smart guy, but he wouldn't want you to be found easily," he surmised, leaving the parking lot farther behind. "So I wouldn't dump the body close to where people would gather." He took a stutter step, then whipped around staring through the tall grass along the path to where it opened up on the concrete. "That assumes that lot was there in the thirties. Damn it."

Torn between doubt and hope about the lot, he took a step forward, then back, then forward again. "Screw it," he growled, continuing around the lake farther and farther from his car. An hour passed. Alex decided he was about halfway around the lake. "OK, so she shows up when someone is in trouble." He wondered, "So...how do I get myself into trouble?" The laugh was loud, causing a scurry through the brush. Startled, he told himself it was only a rabbit or groundhog. The sun was getting higher, and even though there was still a nip to the air, Alex found he was sweating under his jacket. He was also aware he had nothing to drink. This was not a well-planned adventure. Again he was torn as to which direction to take. The distance back was assured from the path he had come; the journey ahead was unknown to him. Sweat beaded on his brow and rolled down his back. Alex was getting nervous. He could feel his feet beginning to hurt. Cursing himself for not being more active, he decided to continue forward.

Another hour found Alex sitting on a smooth boulder rubbing his calves and wishing for a cold drink. It had to be late afternoon now. In his hurry to get moving, he had left his phone in the car. His shirt stuck to his wet skin while his feet burned from use. As the day wore on, it was going to start to get colder. He was dehydrated, wet, tired, and soon to be very cold. "Now would be a good time to show up and get me some help!" he shouted.

"Oh don't be such a baby."

With a yelp, Alex fell backward over the boulder. Crouching, he peered over the rock. In the long reeds at the edge of the lake, he could make out a face. "How long have you been watching me?" he demanded, straightening up. Dusting himself off, he turned back to the face. "Aren't you cold in that water?" he asked through his annoyance.

"No, silly. Unlike you, I don't get cold. And you are going to catch your death if you don't dry out soon. It will be dark before too long." As she spoke, she approached. Alex noticed the reeds didn't move as she made no sound in the water. A look of disappointment clouded her features. "That usually gets a reaction." She pouted.

"Well, Ms. Gay, I have been hanging out with Chloe, and she finds it fun to pop in and out of walls, so…"

Patricia's face brightened as a smile spread across it. "You know who I am." Then a look of dawning clouded her eyes. "Chloe? Chloe Miller? So she's a ghost, too? Oh, she was such a sweet girl. Her family was devastated when she went missing."

Suddenly her eyes hardened. A fire burned behind them, causing Alex to take a step back. "Edgar." She spat as if the word was disgusting to taste. "He killed her, too, didn't he?"

Alex stepped back over the boulder. "Yes," he said sadly. "I am so sorry. Chloe was the first. Then a Brenda Rhodes or maybe you; I don't know."

Stricken, she shook her head while turning her back on him. Gliding a little way back to the water, she spoke. Alex had to strain to hear her. "No, I think I was before Brenda. Is she also a ghost?"

"Yes, a very angry one. She was killed in the woods behind Sterben. Her body is still there." Alex shuffled uncomfortably, trying to think of the best way to ask. Finally he decided straightforward was the best plan. "I'm sorry to ask, but how did you die?"

"You mean how did he kill me? Drowning, of course." She was returning to the shore. "I left work one night. I was just walking home, and I got knocked on the head. I woke up next to Edgar, who was cross-eyed drunk." She laughed, but instantly her face fell. "I tried to get away; I was still dizzy. I fell out of the truck." As she recounted, she began to panic. "He must have noticed. He grabbed my legs. I kicked at him." She looked wildly around. "I got up." She was turning this way and that as if it was happening right then." It was so dark. I could hear the frogs. I tried to run." She grabbed at her head. "Then pain, pain in my head. I knew I was bleeding; it hurt so much. I couldn't see straight. Everything was spinning." She stared down at the water lapping almost silently on the shore. "I fell into the water. I tried to get up, but there was suddenly…there was so much weight on me." She was looking past Alex now. "I couldn't breathe. He was pushing me under the water." Her voice was nothing more than a whisper. "I couldn't breathe. I…I…" She was sobbing now. Alex stood dumbly by, not knowing what to do. "I died." She rubbed at her wrist. "He took my bracelet. The one my grandmother had given me."

"We think that is how he gains his power." Even as the words left his lips, Alex still wondered what power that was. Edgar was dead and, by all accounts, couldn't leave the house. He was trapped just as his victims were. Trapped where they died. *Well, deals with the devil might not be as fulfilling as they appear,* Alex thought. He realized Patricia was watching him again. "Sorry, just trying to understand somethings."

"Like why a boy from an affluent family would kill people and steal things from the bodies." Patricia laughed as she floated back and forth along the lake. "Might be they are just horrible people, no other reason." She flew at him. Alex stumbled back. "Unless you believe the stories about his grandmother being a witch." She laughed at the fear on his face. "No one believes in witches."

"Well, you are a ghost."

She considered him for a long moment. "All right, you have a point there," she conceded.

"Here is the thing..." Alex began as she settled to the ground. "We think there is a stash of stuff in the house that Edgar took from his victims. I think if I can return those items, then you can..." He wasn't sure what to say.

"Move on? Disappear? No longer exist?" She smiled at his discomfort. "It's OK. I have no idea what will happen either. Before I died, I believed in heaven." She was floating back over the bank, not looking at him. "All I know is that hell exists." Kicking the water with a splash, Patricia hung her head. Ghostly tears got lost in the droplets of water running of her transparent face. Alex felt the pain. Wanting to comfort her but unable to reach her out in the water, he stood helpless on the shore.

"I am going to find a..." he began.

Patricia held up a hand to silence him. "You are sweet. If you find a way to release me, I thank you." There followed a shuddering sigh. "For now you need to get someplace warm. Night is falling. The quickest way back to the launch is that way."

Not sure what else to say, he thanked her. Her hand still outstretched, Patricia slowly sank back into the water. A frigid wind hurried Alex along the path. Rounding a clump of thick trees and brush, he saw the parking lot. He had been no more than a thousand feet from his car for the last half hour.

Shivering in the seat, Alex turned up the heater. His phone needed charging, and he had several missed calls from his father. Alex swore to himself, *Edgar will not go unpunished,* as he laid his phone on the bag of books on ghosts and the occult.

UNEXPECTED

While Alex tried to find out how and why Edgar's victims were bound to where they died, work continued on the house. Alex collapsed into a musty overstuffed chair. Wiping his brow, he took a long drink of water. Snow swirled around outside the windows, but the house was warm, almost too warm. A fire was crackling in the fireplace next to the Christmas tree Alex had insisted they put up. The set of Harry Potter books he had given to Chloe was already half-read. He was listening to his father and Chloe shouting back and forth. She was in the walls while he was down in the basement. Together they were running new electric lines. While this was happening, Aaron and Alex had been trying to move the massive cast-iron stove in the kitchen.

"Why can't we just resurface it and leave it where it is?" Aaron complained.

"Because it is not original to the house, and it is rusting to pieces." Alex sighed, handing over a bottle of water. "As much as I would love to leave it there, it's got to go."

"Yeah, yeah, I know."

In the wall behind the chair Alex sat in, Chloe smiled. Aaron loved to complain, while Alex patiently explained why they did things. She had heard this many times over the last few months. It never ceased to entertain her.

"What's the holdup?" Arthur called, shaking Chloe out of her reverie. Focusing her attention back on the cable, she resumed pulling it through the wall. As she went she disconnected the ancient knob and tube wiring that Arthur was pulling back. It made a distinct scraping sound as it was pulled through the old wood and plaster. It took a few moments for her to realize the section of wall she was in was completely clear of the old wiring. The scratching continued.

"Kerlvin?" she softly called. "Is that you?" Standing perfectly still, Chloe waited. Panic rising quickly she said, "Oh god, not rats." She breathed. Her shoulders relaxed. "You're dead. How can they hurt you?" She laughed. It died quickly with a bang from the other side of the wall. "Kerlvin, you are not funny." She dropped the cable as she floated through the wall. Expecting to be in the main living room, she was shocked to find herself in a very small room. Through the dim glow that surrounded her ethereal presence, she could see a star carved into the floor. It was surrounded by symbols she had never seen before. Deep in the shadows, barely visible in the dim light, was what looked like an altar. A chill followed by shaking anxiety crept down Chloe's ghostly spine. "*Alex!*"

Water spurted from Alex's lips, the bottle rolled away, leaving a trail of water through the construction dust. Aaron called after him as Alex called out for Chloe. Turning the corner, she materialized through the wall. "What? What's wrong? Are you OK?" She did not answer, just pointed to the wall.

"I think I found it," she stated simply. Her eyes never wavered from straight ahead. Alex's head swiveled between her face and the blank wall. She didn't look at him. Aaron skidded up next to him.

"What's going on?"

The door to the basement flew open. Arthur thundered up the stairs. "Chloe? Are you all right?"

Chloe seemed to realize everyone was staring at her. She turned slowly to face them. "I found something. Something behind that wall." She pointed to where Alex was already running his hands over the peeling wallpaper. "It was like a shrine or altar or something. I think I found Edgar's tokens," she explained, her voice betraying no emotion. Arthur and Aaron just glanced between each other and Chloe. All the while Alex was searching the wall. Ripping some of the faded paper from the wall like an excited kid on Christmas, he whooped, causing everyone to jump.

"Found it! Yeah, bitch! Thought you could hide from me, mutha..."

"*Alex!*" Chloe and Arthur shouted in unison. Aaron snickered. Alex spun, staring at the others, confused.

"What's the problem? Check this out." He pushed the small knot in one of the exposed panels of old wainscoting. A hollow click filled the hall, followed by a creak. A split appeared in the wall amid a shower of dust. Alex turned slightly to see what the others thought. Aaron shrugged. Arthur was impassive. Only Chloe wore a look of deepest concern and fear. He smiled reassuringly at her. Turning back to the door, Alex felt the desert in his mouth. The tang of the dust and must on his tongue. The secret door protested his efforts with its creaking but was no match for his strength. Light spilled into a space that hadn't seen light in years. The room still held darkness even with the illumination.

"What the hell is that?" Aaron asked over Alex's shoulder. He was pointing at the pentagram on the floor. Alex avoided stepping on the star as he reached for the ornate box set on the brownish stained altar. He ignored the fur, feathers, and bits of bones that littered the foot of the stone. Trembling fingers reach for the box. A deep steeling breath was inhaled as the box was slowly lifted. A clear space in the deep dust stood like a shadow where it had been. As quickly as possible yet painfully slowly and cautiously, it was carried out into the hall. Arthur was now peering into the recess.

"Going to clean the crap out of this space and turn it into a closet." A deep frown crossed his face. "The only hell to come out of here from now on will be stuff to clean the hell out of this house," he growled as the hidden door again was barely seen in the wall closing with a thud.

"Dear God, Dad, that was terrible." Aaron laughed weakly.

THE CLOSED BOX

The box was extremely old and blackened with age and evidence of fire. The ornate lid was carved with strange symbols. Around the body of the box were intricate scenes of suffering and damnation. A discomfort came with just seeing the vessel; touching it was worse. It was cold, like touching death. On the front staring at anyone who dared to try to open the box was a golden skull. Its red-ruby eyes burned brightly. Looking at it Alex felt like it was watching him, daring him to try to open it. Cautiously he ran a finger along the face. It moved slightly under his touch. His mouth was a desert while his throat burned. He tried to swallow. Every breath felt like dust in his lungs. Feeling the eyes on his back, he moved the skull. It slid smoothly up, revealing fangs on the top and bottom. In the middle of the mouth was a small keyhole.

"Are you freaking kidding me?" Aaron growled, snatching the box from Alex's grip. Jamming the claw end of a hammer between the top and bottom, he tried to force it open. He stood it on end, stood on the large half, and tried again to pry it open. Now Arthur and Aaron had a crowbar. Metal clanged as they tried to force the bar into the crack. The lid did not budge while barely a scratch appeared on the ancient wood.

Ignoring Alex's protests, Aaron tried the saw, a drill, a hacksaw, and pounded the box with a sledgehammer. He was about to take it outside to run it over with the truck when Alex grabbed it. "I don't know what the hell is keeping this shut, but look at it!" He held it out. Nothing made even the slightest mark on the surface. "We have to use the key, or there is no way in to this thing."

"We were lucky to find that thing. How the hell are we going to find the key for it?" Aaron shouted. Alex and Aaron turned as their father grumbled something as he headed to the door. He turned back to the boys as he turned the knob.

"Chloe, I'm counting on you to keep these two from doing anything stupid with that thing." He nodded to the box. "I'll be back in a half hour." The door closed on three confused faces.

Twenty minutes later found the three of them staring at the impenetrable box. Holding up a chisel, Aaron asked, "What if I...?"

"No," Chloe and Alex replied, annoyance clear in each. Aaron was crestfallen. Frustrated, he wandered down the hall. Inspecting the ancient grandfather clock that ticked away the moments, he grumbled.

"Dad will be back any minute." He spun to face them, a manic gleam in his eye. "Let me have just one more whack at it!"

Before a response could be made, the front door swung wide, aided by a cold wind that scattered leaves across the foyer. Lightning flashed, silhouetting a man in the opening. Alex fell back out of his chair, Chloe squeaked in fear, while Aaron cried out, "What a bunch of babies." Arthur grumbled as he shut the door behind him. His hands held an ancient book and a leather pouch.

"Um, just startled, that's all." Alex got guiltily to his feet. "Say, what have you got there, Dad?"

Arthur moved closer to the box but did not answer his son. Alex looked over his father's shoulder at the tome he had set beside the wooden casket. The binding creaked as Arthur carefully opened the yellowed pages.

"Is that...a spell book?" Chloe breathed.

Alex, Aaron, and Chloe stood entranced, waiting with a collective held breath. Arthur's eyes rose slowly from the musty page to meet theirs. "What?" he asked as a quizzical look crossed his face. Metal tools clinked free from the leather pouch. "No, this is Granddad's manual on blacksmithing. My granddad's, I mean. What the hell would I be doing with a spell book?" He shook his head at his sons. Chloe suppressed a laugh by trying to turn it into a cough.

"Good try." Aaron frowned. "Since when do ghosts cough?"

Laughing now, Chloe replied, "It could happen."

Alex ignored the conversation behind him as he watched his father work. Excitement built with each click in the tiny lock. Every time Arthur seemed to think he had it, the box remained resolutely shut. Suddenly Aaron cried out, "Blood! I bet it needs a blood offering. I mean, that is what this type of thing needs in the movies, right?" He grabbed a box cutter and began to inspect his fingers, trying to determine which one to cut. The blade began to press into the flesh when...

"Got it. Put the knife away, dummy." Arthur held the open box out to them.

CONTENTS

Chloe, Alex, and Aaron stood stock-still, staring at the open lid. From their angle they could not see what the box held. Aaron was the first to approach, Alex close behind. Taking the box from his father, Alex carefully set it down on a small, spindly table. The three men looked at the contents while Chloe hovered well back from them.

"What is this?" Aaron wondered. holding up some rolled-up burlap.

"Careful," Alex warned, taking the material from Aaron. Fibers scattered from the deteriorating cloth. Cautiously he laid it on the table, slowly unrolling it. A delicate ring appeared, its silver tarnished, but the green gem still shone magnificently. Next to be revealed was a fine golden bracelet, then a large ring with a family crest engraved in it. Alex held his breath as he continued to unroll the fragile fabric. Several military medals clinked out, but Alex did not know their origin. The last secret to be revealed was a silk ribbon. It was stained in several areas. Realizing Chloe wasn't nearby, Alex turned to see her staring at the floor.

With a shaking hand, Alex held out the ribbon to her. Aaron and Arthur stood well back. She could feel the sorrow in their eyes. "Is this yours?" Alex asked.

Chloe's fingers caressed the ribbon. "I think so. It was nothing special. It was in..." Her hand slipped into the pocket of her coat, retrieving the ghostly twin. Alex placed the ribbon overtop of the phantom one. Just like the earring and the shoe, Chloe became a bit more whole. "This is not my necklace," she stated, a single tear leaking down her cheek. "He took so much from me." Before Alex could say anything, she disappeared, her soft crying slowly fading down the hall to the conservatory.

"Damn it!" Alex punched his hand. "I thought for sure we'd find it!"

"I know, man, and I'm sorry, but we need to figure this shit out." Aaron held the medals out to Alex and Arthur.

"That is a Vietnam service medal; I have one of those," Arthur explained, holding up the slightly greenish brass medal. "I think this is a Korean one." He held up a blue ribbon with another round medallion hanging from it.

Alex puzzled at the medals, scratching his chin. "That makes no sense. Edgar didn't serve, and I think he was dead by the time Vietnam started, maybe even Korea, so what the hell?"

"What are these last three?" Aaron held them up to the light.

"That is a World War Two victory medal, an American Campaign medal, and this last one is an Asiatic Pacific Campaign medal." Arthur examined the ribbons closely.

"So what, Edgar started killing soldiers?" Aaron asked.

"Only if he was a time traveler. Remember, he was dead by the mid-fifties." Alex replied.

"So where did this stuff come from?" Aaron demanded.

"We know Chloe has to stay in this house," Arthur interrupted. "We don't actually know Edgar has to." They found themselves staring at the ceiling, looking toward the back bedroom. "I mean, what if, since he's the killer and the one who made the deal, he isn't stuck here?"

"Alex, maybe you need to find Chloe and that little demon thing," Aaron whispered. "See if you can get some answers."

Alex nodded, only half-listening, his mind searching for reasons for the medals to be there and how he would find out how to return them. A thought hit him so hard, he threw out a hand to steady himself against the wall. Alex breathed his idea as if speaking it could make it true. "What if Edgar possessed people?" Alex fell back against the wall, legs shaking. "Europe, the Pacific, Asia…How in the hell could we even find his victims from wars?" He rubbed his eyes, distracted by the insurmountable task that may lie ahead.

"I'm sorry."

Alex jumped. Doubled over, hands on his knees, he tried to recall his breathing. "Oh. man, Chloe, you startled me."

"I'm sorry for that. too." She smiled sadly at him. "I didn't know what to expect when the box was opened." She paused, confused. "I mean I was happy that I might be free, terrified that I was going to be, then so disappointed. I don't know." She was searching his eyes for understanding.

"I know how you feel." Alex sighed, looking away. "I wasn't sure I was ready to lose you…" A blush crept over his face. "I mean…um," he stuttered. She looked shocked for a moment. Alex tried to apologize but was met with a shy smile. "Chloe, I…"

"You humans are so disgusting," Kerlvin sneered. "I guess this would make you a necro…no…phantasmaphile." He snapped his long bony fingers as the word came to him. A spark shot up; the air held the taint of sulfur.

INFORMATION

Chloe and Alex sprang apart at the intrusion. "Kerlvin," Alex growled.

"Not the nicest today, are we?" the demon replied, unconcerned, a sharp black claw digging at something in his teeth. Chloe looked away in disgust as Kerlvin flicked away a small rat arm. "I see you found the box." He glanced back toward it. "Oh good, you found a way to open it." He inspected his black sharp claws. "No one was dumb enough to give it blood, I see. That would have been disastrous," he snickered.

Chloe looked concerned. "What would have happened?"

"Oh, nothing much," He grinned, it wasn't a pleasant grin. "The box would just gain an appetite. An appetite that could be sated only by death." He reveled in the looks on their faces. "The death of the one foolish enough to give it blood in the first place...poor simple Aaron." The cackle that followed turned Alex's stomach.

"Well, I'm glad nobody gave it blood then," Alex replied angrily.

Chloe floated between them. She could see Kerlvin's eyebrow raised and knew he was taunting Alex. "Thank you for helping us find the box." She calmed.

"Oh, I did no such thing. In fact..." He looked to where the severed rat arm lay. "The one who did lead you was delicious." The look on Chloe's face brought the sickening grin back to his. "Although now that you have it, I am guessing you have some questions."

"Well, yes, we do," Alex confirmed, stepping in front of Chloe. The leer she was receiving from Kerlvin made him uncomfortable. "I think all we have to do is return some of these things to their owners, right?" Alex frowned at the noncommittal response from the demon. "We have two problems, though." He waited until Kerlvin gave him his attention. "Chloe's necklace isn't here, and we have no idea what these medals mean or how we return them. I mean they are from all over..." Alex faltered at the clicking of a sharp black claw on the wooden floor. Kerlvin seemed to have completely lost interest. He examined the claws on his left hand while the ones on his right foot scratched at the hardwood floor.

"Can you please help us?" Chloe asked, ignoring the warning look from Alex.

"Well, since you asked so nicely." Kerlvin laughed. "No." He continued his inspection.

"That's OK. I am starting to like it here." Chloe shrugged. "I mean I have no place I need to be. I could spend another seventy years here." She smiled around at the room. "One hundred and forty years." Her eyes returned to the demon. He pretended to not be interested, but Alex could see Kerlvin was looking at her over his knuckles. Chloe ran a ghostly hand along the rough plaster. "I am feeling at home here. I guess it really is my home." She twirled, arms outstretched. "I have missed having a home, being around those like me." Alex was about to point out there weren't any other ghosts around when Kerlvin broke in.

"Yeah, yeah, I can see what you are doing." His hand fell to his side. With a huge sigh as if it were a great inconvenience, he began to explain. "You're right about the items. Return them to the victims, and they will be released." He held up his four-fingered hand to halt Alex's question. "The medals are the easiest." He looked from one confused face to the other. Clearly enjoying their lack of understanding, Kerlvin allowed the silence to drag. Finally he stated. "The items he took were trophies, right?" The demon waited. Alex looked at Chloe. She looked back at Alex. Both shrugged and looked back to Kerlvin. He rolled his eyes. "He took trophies..." Blank stares. "Trophies are prizes..." He waved his hand in a small circle encouraging them to get the idea. He huffed. "Prizes can be given out as medals..."

"So we give the medals back to the government?" Alex asked.

Kerlvin slapped his own forehead and growled, "Dumb as his brother, that one."

"They were rewards for killing," Chloe whispered. "So if we destroy those awards..." She hesitated. Kerlvin waved his hands toward himself, encouraging her to continue. "He has no trophy...So those souls can rest."

"Oh, thank God!" Kerlvin gasped dramatically, flourishing his hands. "Well, not really. Me and the big guy don't actually see eye to eye on many things." He shrugged.

Alex wasn't listening. He was hurrying back to the box. Scooping up the medals, he glanced around as if the best way to destroy them would jump out to present itself.

Back down the hall, Kerlvin and Chloe stood in uncomfortable silence. "Thank you for helping us," she whispered.

Kerlvin threw up his hands in defense. "Hey, hey, I haven't helped at all. I couldn't even if I wanted to. If you followed scratching, that was on you. If you understood that trophies could be medals, then hey." He shrugged. "I'm a demon. I am not going to help anyone."

"Well, I am thankful we found this information." She threw him a quick smile as she hurried to Alex. In spite of himself,

Kerlvin smiled, too. It quickly slipped into disgust as his wings unfurled, and he took off toward the second floor.

RETURN OF THE FEELING

Filled with confused annoyance, Kerlvin landed with a thud outside Edgar's room. Pacing, he berated himself for allowing Chloe's smile to affect him. "If the master knew. If the master knew, oh, I'd be in for it," he grumbled. "What is the matter with you?" he demanded of the reflection in the filthy, tarnished mirror that hung opposite the dusty window in the hall. As he stared at the red face and black horns, Kerlvin began to notice the mirror was shaking.

Deep in the gloom of the undisturbed bedroom, a feeling was growing. Edgar was aware of his body for the first time in years. He could see only the black tendrils of smoke that composed his spirit, but he felt his feet, his legs, his arms, and his fingers. He felt the emptiness on the ring finger of his right hand. Its absence burned his hand. There it was. The anger, the hatred, the loathing returned. His red eyes flew to the door. Around the frame was a barrier of flame. He was a being like smoke and burning rage; he felt no fear of the fire. Edgar slammed into the flames. Light exploded through the room, causing him to pause. Moldy bedding lay torn and strewn over the filthy floor. Dead mice, rats, and a bird lay among the scattered feces and fallen plaster. The state of his once-elegant room shocked him. A howl exploded from within the billowing, churning black smoke. Light exploded as Edgar hit the barrier again.

Out in the back of the property a wail of bitter abandonment scattered birds from the trees. An angry, biting wind threw leaves, twigs, and dirt into the air. The desiccated corpse that was her body lay, brown, white, and withered, on the ground. Staring from the black holes where her eyes once were, the anger and sadness returned. "Where is my ring?" she demanded of the body. A blast of wind knocked the skull loose from the dried tendons holding it on. "Where is my grandmother's ring?" she screamed. The rotten hands flew apart, joining the rest of the detritus blowing, swirling among the trees.

Farther away, the cold waters of the lake reverberated with sobbing. A feeling of defeated uselessness covered the area. Patricia lay close to the shore. Her tears flowed into the surrounding waters. One ghostly hand caressed the wrist of her other arm. "I couldn't stop him," she wailed. "He took my life and took my bracelet." She floated just below the surface. "My mother gave that to me on Christmas when I was thirteen." She was sinking into the lake and into her own despair. "It was the year we didn't think we'd have a Christmas. Father was out of work, and Mother had been sick." Her guilt and sadness settled over her as her ghost settled into the mud inside the bones embedded in the bottom of the lake.

Across Europe and Asia, townspeople, villagers, and farmers listened in terror to the sounds of dying. Screams of agony, hatred, and sorrow filled the lands that had once been battlefields. Just as suddenly as the crying started, it was silenced. A feeling of peace and calm returned to the areas.

Chloe felt the pain, the loneliness, and utter sorrow fill her. She watched from the window as Arthur and Aaron used the acetylene torch on the medals. The ribbons turned to ash in an instant. A whispered of sadness escaped as they burned. When each medal was reduced to a molten lump, a cry of agony broke the night air. Alex stood behind his father, watching as the trophies disintegrated. When the hiss of the torch was silenced, they heard the screaming from the woods.

PUT TO REST

Chloe moved aside as the three men reentered the house.
Alex reached into the box, retrieving the last of its contents.
Their excitement and trepidation overshadowed all else. Chloe
tried to smile encouragingly as Alex explained what was
happening. "I swear it worked. There were all these sounds,
screams and crying, then...I don't know...peace, I guess. I could
just tell it worked." Alex's face was so hopeful that Chloe was
sure he was right.

Aaron thundered through the hall grabbing jackets. "Come
on, we should do this together." He tossed Alex his coat; Arthur
was already struggling into his. "Remember, this lady is already
angry."

Arthur called to his youngest son, "Come on; we should
check on the girl in the lake as soon as we are done here." The
door slammed, followed by heavy footfalls on the wooden
porch.

"Are you OK?" Alex asked. Chloe smiled, shaking off his
concern.

"I'm fine. You go set them free."

"We'll find your necklace. I promise." He apologized. The
door swung open. His brother was now beckoning. "We'll figure
this out," he promised. Chloe nodded her understanding, not
trusting her voice to cry or shout in anguish. The door shut, and
the footfalls faded as they disappeared into the increasing
darkness. Chloe stood listening to the steady thumping when
she realized she was alone in the house.

Alex hurried after his brother, pulling the ring from Aaron's
hand. The beam from their father's flashlight bounced ahead of

them. "Come on! We can't let Dad get there first," Alex warned, increasing his pace. On the edge of the small clearing, he skidded to a halt. The howl of the wind increased while the leaves whipped at his face.

Brenda stood in the middle of a tempest. Around her swirled deadly missiles of bone, branches, and stones. Arthur's flashlight illuminated the specter. Her hair floated out around her, her arms outstretched, tattered clothes flying in the tornado's winds. Over the howl of the wind they could clearly hear her wailing anger.

"OK, how do we do this?" Aaron called to his brother over the noise.

"No idea!" Alex shouted. He had caught her attention.

An emaciated finger pointed accusingly at him. "You! Where is my ring!" she cried, flying to the edge of the swirling mass.

"I...I...I have it here." Alex held out his hand; the ring lay in his palm. Silence filled the dale punctuated by only the sounds of detritus hitting the earth. Alex took a tentative step forward, hand outstretched. Brenda's fingers shook as she reached toward the small piece of jewelry.

"My ring." Her ghostly hand shook as she reached out. "It's been gone so long," Brenda whispered. Aaron's hands grabbed onto Alex's shoulders, ready to pull him back. Brenda's finger brushed the gold. The ring lifted, weightless, from Alex's hand. Brenda slipped it onto her finger. Immediately she began to glow softly. A warm, kind smile spread across her face as her body began to solidify. Voices called from the distance.

"Brenda! Brenda, where are you?" Brenda stared around in a frantic search, trying to find the source of the calls.

Tears sprang to her eyes. "Dad?" she called. "Dad! I'm here! Help me."

"Brenny, it's your mother; where are you?" Two spirits appeared at the tree line, a woman and a man holding hands, beaming across at Brenda.

"Oh my God, we found you." The spirit that had to be Brenda's mother spoke as she sunk to her knees.

"We've been searching so long." Brenda's father smiled at her through his tears. Brenda crossed slowly to her parents.

"You were looking for me?"

"We never stopped," her mother explained as tears streamed down her face. Brenda walked into their arms. There was a flash of pure-white light. Blinded for a moment, Alex slowly lowered his arm from covering his eyes. The three men were alone. As the realization of what had just occurred sank in, they stood smiling at one another. Suddenly all three dropped to a crouch. A scream of unholy anger boomed overhead.

"W...was that Edgar?" Aaron asked shakily.

"I hope so," Alex replied with a satisfied nod. "Come on; let's get this back to Patricia," he exclaimed, holding out the bracelet. "Let's hope this one hurts that bastard even more." Twenty minutes later found them standing on the shore of the lake. Alex had found the rock he had been sitting on when he had spoken to Patricia. Now he was standing in front of it, shouting her name. Something was creeping over them. Arthur could feel it, and by the looks his sons were giving him, so could they. A feeling of helplessness, of despair, crept into their souls.

"Why isn't she answering?" Aaron whispered. "Oh man, this is hopeless. We should just call it a night and go home."

Alex looked over at his brother, his shoulders slumped. "Yeah maybe your right; I mean, what can we do?"

Arthur was nodding in agreement, then suddenly became angry. "Damn it, boys; snap out of it. We can't give up." He pulled Aaron over to Alex and held both men on the shoulder. "Don't give in to despair. We have to help Patricia."

"What can you do?" Patricia asked as she rose slowly from the water. "I couldn't stop him. He killed me, took my bracelet, and left me to rot down there." She pointed to the smooth surface of the water. "I've tried so many times to help others since then," she said sadly. "Sometimes it worked, like with you, Alex. Most times I think I just made it worse." She was crying now. "I didn't want to die. I had plans." She slowly glided over the water toward them. "I didn't want anyone else to die unfulfilled, but when someone did..." She was right in front of them. "When someone did die here"—she looked back over the glassy surface—"I hoped they would stay here. So I could have a friend." She looked imploringly at them. "Does that make me a bad person?"

Alex stepped forward. "No, no, it does not. It just makes you lonely." A spark ignited in his chest as he rummaged in a pocket. "I have something that might help." His fingers finally grasped what he was searching for. Carefully he produced the fine silver bracelet. He held it out to her. She, in turn, held out her wrist. When it was clasped in place, the call of many voices met their ears.

"My friends!" Patricia gasped.

"Pat! Where did you go?"

"We couldn't find you."

"Come on; we have so much to show you." Patricia disappeared, surrounded by a group of happy laughing people. They seemed thrilled to have her back. The feeling of joy was infectious. Once the flash faded, a pained angry howl broke overhead.

"Edgar." Aaron smiled.

Alex's satisfied smirk changed instantly to a frown. "Chloe!" he shouted, sprinting for the car.

KNOCKING ON EVIL'S DOOR

Kerlvin slowly approached the door. He could hear
something coming from inside, a pounding. Scratching at his
chin, he placed a pointed ear to the wood. "Surely he isn't trying
to break through my barrier?" the demon muttered. The door
shuddered in its frame. Dust fell from the moldings; a piece of
plaster smashed painfully on Kerlvin's head. Angrily he rubbed
at the spot while looking at the hole in the ceiling. Already
annoyed, he heard Chloe's voice calling up the stairs. He took
one step toward the stairs when it happened. The door
exploded outward, slamming the demon into the opposite wall.
He slid down the surface slowly, his eyes slipping out of focus.
The great boiling cloud of black crossed his vision before
consciousness left him.

Chloe leaped back from the bottom stair at the sound of
splintering wood. She rushed to the box only to find it empty.
Panicked, she turned toward the conservatory. A cry escaped
her throat. She was trapped, her way being blocked by the
billowing cloud of anger that Edgar had become. Burning red
eyes bore into hers. A gaping mouth opened, revealing the
flames of hell. "Where is my ring?" a voice of gravel being
crushed under granite demanded.

Terrified, Chloe backed away. Then anger of her own boiled
to the surface. She stopped, hands on her hips, glaring at him.
"Where is my necklace?" she demanded. Edgar stopped his
advance. The flames in his eyes dimmed slightly. The mouth
took on a grimace as if confused.

"You took my ring. You haunt me. You won't let me rest!"
Edgar thundered.

Now it was Chloe's turn to be confused. "Haunt you?" she asked. The anger overtook the confusion. "You killed me!" she cried, equaling him in volume. They stood staring at each other, her pale-blue eyes searching his red fiery ones. Chloe squeaked out in terror. A black tendril shot at her, barely missing her face as she ducked away.

"Give me back my ring!" he roared.

Ducking behind the sofa, she called back. "I don't have your ring. Alex does." She clamped a hand over her mouth. She had not intended to tell him that. Now that it was out, she had to do something. "An...and...and he won't give it back." She moved farther away. "Un...until you give me back my necklace," she explained in a voice that sounded much braver than she felt. The sofa flew away, smashing into the small table set up in the middle of the room.

"Who is Alex?" Edgar advanced on her. "How do you know he has my ring?"

Chloe danced out of reach. Edgar's smoky hands kept flying out to grab her. "It's an ugly gold thing with a bird and a sword on it," she explained, eyeing the doorway. She thought of the safety of the conservatory. The thought hit her, was it actually safe?

"Give it back!" he roared.

"I don't have it!" she shot back. She was almost there.

"Give me my ring, and leave me alone!"

Chloe paused. Edgar's voice sounded pleading, sad, and pained. The pause was all Edgar needed. Smoke enveloped her, pinning her arms to her sides, those burning red eyes inches from her face. She could feel the fire from them, the heat from the flames in his mouth, flames that burned away his humanity. "It was an accident," he hissed at her. "I was drunk." The coils tightened; she felt the pain. "I didn't know what had happened until we were back here."

"I...I was still alive when you dumped me down that well." She fought against the increasing pressure.

"You were dead either way." His gripped loosened slightly. "I didn't mean to do it. It was an accident." The pain returned, crushing her. "Why can't you understand that? Why can't you forget it already?"

Struggling to free her arms, Chloe fought, "I'm stuck here because you murdered me. How can I forget that I'm trapped with the man who killed me?" Her hand sprung free. She quickly tried to claw at his eyes. Her fingers swirled the smoke around, but Edgar still cried out in pain. She was free, her ears filled with his pained screams. Chloe was running down the hall. Her feet were hitting the ground, her legs burning. The sensation was startling as was the pain the shot through her knees, wrists, and face as they slammed into the floor. Long ropes of smoke pulled her back down the hall. Her fingernails scratched deep into the floorboards. The pain was too intense as the nails separated from the fingers. Chloe's screams mixed with Edgar's.

She was flung into the air. For a moment she was weightless, inches from the ceiling. The moment was gone. She slammed back to the floor. A tooth flew free from her mouth. She watched it fly in slow motion. She was aware of the hole in her gum, the blood filling her mouth.

"It." She was in the air again.

"Was." She smashed down. Pain exploding through her like the day she was hit.

"An." Back in the air screaming in fear.

"*Accident!*" She was dazed in pain. Her arm didn't work, nor did her legs. Warm, sticky blood covered her lips and chin.

Edgar regarded her for a moment. "Looks like even in death, I can hurt you. I don't want to hurt you." Edgar sounded apologetic again. "I just want my ring and to be left alone." He was pacing now. "No town girls reminding me I killed them." The mass around the head shook. "No demons reminding me I'm destined for hell." He looked down at her as she tried to pull herself back down the hall. "As if this wasn't hell enough." He flipped her over, so she could see his eyes. "I'm going to ask you one last time." He stomped on her already-shattered leg. Yelling over her screams, he asked again. "Where is my ring?"

Through her streaming eyes, she saw him drop to his knees. Her eyes were glued to the heavy fist that hung over her head. She knew the blow was coming. She could already feel the pain. What would it be like to die again? Would she come back again, or would that be it? She wanted to see Alex again. Her heart leaped at the sound of the front door opening. Hopeful, she turned toward the sound. Her heart froze. A tall man wearing a very expensive suit stood in the foyer. He had dark hair and looked young and athletic. Slowly he turned his handsome face to the scene in the sitting room. His eyes traveled slowly from the broken girl on the floor to the swirling hatred standing over her.

Edgar's grip was gone as he stood staring at the newcomer. Chloe pushed herself up against the wall. She stared at the man as well, disbelieving her eyes. Now she was looking back to Edgar as the smoke disappeared, vanishing back to reveal a short, balding, overweight man. He had greasy hair and a poor complexion. His mouth hung open, displaying rotten and missing teeth. "Richard," he whispered.

THE RETURN

"Oh, good heavens, Edgar, you still have no idea how to treat a woman." Richard laughed as he approached Chloe. Crouching, he lifted her face. He looked into her tear-filled eyes. "It just never ends for you, does it?" he said sympathetically as he stroked her hair lightly. Waving his hands slowly over her, Richard looked back over his shoulder with a wink at his brother. Chloe felt the bones mend, the torn tissue heal, and the pain cease. Weakly, she was able to regain her feet. "Ah, that's better, isn't it?" Richard smiled. "My dear brother here was never a gentleman."

Edgar's face crumpled. In a matter of seconds, wave after wave of emotion crossed its surface. Running from stunned to anger to hideous hate and landing on rage. "Why are you here?" He exploded. "Why do you look the same?" He was pacing now, shaking his head, arms flailing. "Why aren't you old or dead!" he demanded, advancing on his brother.

"Oh, poor, poor, Edgar. You never were very bright." Richard laughed. Chloe was slowly edging toward the door. A yelp left her lips as her feet left the ground. She was whipped through the air. The yelp became a scream until she smashed into Edgar. She was pressed against his side. She struggled to distance herself. It felt as if steel bands held her in place; she couldn't move. "Oh, you don't want to leave." Richard turned to them smiling. "You'll miss the touching family reunion." Richard's smile was not pleasant. It distorted his handsome features, turning them cruel. Behind Richard a cold wind whipped through the foyer. The front door banged hard into the wall.

"Who the hell are you?" Alex demanded.

"Ah, guests to the party." Richard's cold smile was turned on Alex. "Allow me to introduce myself. I am Richard Davis, the master of this house," Richard explained with a small bow. "I have returned because someone has been meddling in affairs that are not his to meddle in," he explained. His attention had returned to Edgar and Chloe.

"I do believe you are mistaken. This house belongs to us," Arthur shouted, pushing his way past his son.

Richard turned, glaring at the three men. "It is with great displeasure that I return to this house." His voice, barely above a whisper, carried throughout the halls.

"So sorry you had to be summoned back," Alex replied in mock courtesy. "But you see your brother has been a very bad boy and needs..." Alex was cut short by Richard's laugh.

"Oh, my dear boy, you have no idea what Edgar has or hasn't done." Richard's attention was now completely on Alex and his family. Chloe felt the bond attaching her to Edgar ease. Richard was distracted. "As for the owners of this house, your family was expelled once. I don't think it will be hard to do it again." As he spoke he did not notice Chloe edging away from Edgar. Nor did he see the swirling cloud starting to form around his brother. Chloe first tried to disappear through the wall but found it to be a solid barrier. With one eye on Edgar and the other on Richard, she had almost reached the doorway. "I think not!" Richard shouted. Chloe flew into the air, hanging immobile. Edgar took two steps toward them. In an instant he was through to the floor in the front room. The French doors that separated the front room from the foyer slammed shut. Edgar's swirling blackness boiled against the glass. "Right, now that we have these two, um, restrained, maybe I can explain what is going on here." Richard's ugly smile returned.

"I think we have a pretty good idea of what is going on," Alex cut in. "Edgar made a deal with a demon. He killed Chloe, Brenda, and Patricia, and who knows how many other people."

"Yes, yes, interesting theory." Richard nodded in agreement. "A few problems with it, though, aren't there?" He approached the small table along the wall. His fingers brushed the twisted burned remnants of the service medals. "Such as these, and of course, if he made such a deal, what were the benefits and conditions?"

"I...conditions...benefits...I, well, he had to kill innocent girls in order to..." Alex faltered. A look of confusion began to spread across his face. Even as he said it, he could remember the problems and holes in what he said. Richard's eyebrow rose expectantly. His eyes taunted Alex to explain. "To save the mill and...and he somehow...gave you the benefits like long life by the looks of you," Alex finished lamely.

"It's true, dear Chloe was the first. She died for many reasons, not the least of which was to seal the pact with the demon."

"What other possible reason would he have to kill her?" Alex demanded.

"She was young, pretty." Richard shrugged. "And disrespected my brother."

Alex scoffed at this. "I doubt that was the first time that happened. So he killed her because she embarrassed him?"

"Oh my dear boy, you misunderstand. My brother was a fool. Yes, he was always disregarded by the local girls." Richard laughed. "I mean, he had tried to impugn the reputation of one of those silly schoolgirls the week before." The memory brought a leering smile to the cruel face. "You see, young Chloe was bright and pure. She was the very last word in kindness and hope." Richard turned to Chloe, who still hung immobile in the air. "I knew she would be missed by family and friends. She was well liked, but then my brother tried to pick her up." His evil smile returned to Alex. "It was just too easy. Get Edgar something to drink. Wait until he no longer knew his name and run the poor girl down."

"Wait, were you with him? You could have saved her!" Alex shouted.

Richard's laughing was loud and long. "Oh my God, you still don't understand, do you?" He tried to get control of his breathing. "Edgar didn't kill Chloe; I did." There was no hiding the glee in his tone.

"You didn't care about your brother! You used him," Alex stammered.

"All this time that fool believed he killed those three girls." Richard walked up to Chloe. He looked into her frightened eyes. He could see the fear turning to anger. He reached out to her. She tried to recoil. His hand found her arm. With a cruel flick of his wrist, she spun in the air. "Oh, this is so delicious." His lips curled, revealing pointy teeth. "Chloe bounced off the truck all broken and battered. There I was in Edgar's ear telling him what to do." He pranced over the glass-contained spirit. "When he woke up in the woods after we went hunting and that diner girl was dead, it was me who told him to hide the body. I stood on that foolish girl's back, drowning her. Edgar woke up soaking wet, seeing the body floating in the shallows. I convinced him what was best." Richard twirled, arms outstretched. "Then I helped Edgar sink her into the mud." He was back at the French doors tapping on the glass. "That guilt, anger, and remorse ate him up as it was feeding that pathetic little demon they sent to watch over me." He waved a hand, forcing Arthur and Aaron onto the small ottoman. "Sit. I saw you trying to grab weapons.

The boy and I will continue this without your useless interruptions."

Struggling against the invisible force holding him down, Arthur roared, "This is my home and my family! I demand you leave this..."

"Silence, old fool!" Richard thundered. "I took this house from your family. It was my magic that caused your misfortunes. I took that power from that old witch in the forest." A red glow rose from Richard's shoulders as he continued to scream, the smile no longer on his face, replaced with pure malice. "I took your home! I destroyed your family once. You will witness as I do it again." Richard's breathing was fast and heavy. He closed his eyes, inhaling deeply. The glow faded. "Now, young man, let us sit." Alex knew he could move but had no idea what he could possibly do against this adversary. Richard waved him over to the table. "Come here. I got these for service in wars. I was in Europe, the Pacific, and all over Southeast Asia. It is so easy in war." He turned, face full of delight. "And you thought what? Edgar's ghost joined up?" Alex felt his face burn. "Dear Chloe is special. It all came down to her. So pure, so innocent. I've kept her all these years."

Behind the glass, Edgar's world was imploding. Disbelief fought with rage. "All this time!" he tried to shout, coming out in an incoherent roar. "I never killed anyone." Within his cloud, Edgar sank to the floor. "All this time." Pounding his fists against his head, he tried to remember each death. The heavy crunch of metal like a boom in his head woke him. He was in the passenger seat. He could still hear her crying and the clinking of the bottles. Hugging himself, he could feel the cold of the ground. It was the blast of a rifle that woke him. Then the horror at the sight of that girl lying in the leaves. His sweat ran in rivulets like he had just surfaced from the lake. There she was, facedown in the water, Richard at his side asking what he had done and helping hide the body. Richard was always there to help hide the body. Richard was always sober and always there. Edgar flew at the door, fists slamming into the glass. His world spun. He flew through a vortex of memories and pain.

1947

Whispering in the dark. Edgar could hear voices. There was movement somewhere, a dark scurry of claws scratching along stone. "Not the death I had planned," Richard's voice called from far away. "But a soul is a soul." Richard laughed. Edgar could feel a tug on his little finger. The pinkie ring he wore there was being stolen. It held the family crest.

"You know I never want to be without that," he tried to shout. As the oldest it was his right to take it to the grave. "Richard! Leave it alone," he cried. Richard was laughing. There was someone else in the room. The presence emanated evil. Waves of malice, terror, and sorrow pulsed from the creature. Edgar knew it wasn't a man. The smell of sulfur burned his nose. Trembling, Edgar turned his head to the blackness. What he saw threatened to throw his mind further into madness. Through dim glowing firelight, horns rose up. Blacker than the darkness that surrounded them, they transitioned into red skin of the pointed head. The head sat atop a huge crimson body that turned furry and goatlike at the waist. Edgar shut his eyes tightly.

"I'm dreaming. I know I am. Please let me wake up. God, please let me wake up," Edgar cried. His pleas were met with laughter. Richard and the presence were laughing at him. "Please, Richard, help me." Edgar could see the outline of his brother silhouetted in a doorway. Reaching out, he screamed. "The devil is here. He is here to drag me to hell. I've been killed, and I am going to hell! Help me. You said you would always help me!"

The devil was laughing. It was a deep, terrifying sound devoid of all mirth. Edgar knew it was the devil. He could hear the minions scurrying around in the darkness. The deep laughter was growing louder. Finally, a voice filled with menace broke through. There was still shrill cackling all around. "Oh, yes, you will go to hell, but I am not here to take you." The devil laughed again. "Poor Richard has not fulfilled the terms."

"What do you mean?" Richard shouted from the door. "I delivered a soul within the time required." Richard took a step back. Light caught his face. It was disfigured, burned, and scarred. He ran a hand over it, crying out. "I delivered a soul!"

"This one is far too damaged. I require a whole soul, an innocent soul." Dark flame rose, black and deep crimson. "You have given me something that is already mine."

"I had him killed! I took the trophy. I fulfilled the terms." Richard's argument was cut off.

"You have failed me!" the devil roared. "Do you think to trick me? Do you think I shall be merciful?" The laughing was gone, replaced by growls. A sea of hungry eyes flowed out of the flames. Edgar could feel their weight on his bed; their claws scratched and stabbed as they crept over him. He tried to move. He was paralyzed. He tried to call out. Angry blood-covered teeth snapped in his face. Black eyes reflected his terrified features. Red-faced with a long nose and black horns, the minion pushed a long, thin finger tipped with a black claw against Edgar's lips.

"It's master's time to talk," it hissed.

A tear rolled out of Edgar's eye. The creature on his chest pulled and pressed his flesh like a cat bedding down. Claws dug into his skin as the full weight of the demon curled up on him. It hissed out words Edgar couldn't understand.

"Do you think you can dictate the terms once the deal is signed?" The devil continued to roar.

"I did what the contract said," Richard pleaded. "I have given you a soul."

"You did not claim this one. You know this is a condemned. This does not fulfill the deal." The voice lowered. "You may yet be spared." The horrible laughing returned. "I shall leave this one for my pet. Would you like that, Kerlvin?" the devil cooed. "I will take the murderer." Edgar felt a rush of hot wind blow across his face. Richard yelled in fright as Lawrence, the man he sent to help Edgar run the mill and to kill him, rose up. Now Lawrence was screaming, grabbing, and clawing at Richard, the doorframe, the walls, anything he could. He flew over Edgar into the hand of the devil. Lawrence's screams ceased in a ball of flame erupting from the beast's hand.

"I have half of your debt. You will bring me another, and all will be forgiven." Another wave of heat passed over Edgar. Richard was running a hand over his smooth young features.

"I will." Richard bowed. The light from the doorway was gone. The flames disappeared. Edgar was left in blackness. The weight and pain of the thing on his chest did not change.

Morning came. Edgar lay in his bed not feeling the hangover he was sure to be fighting later. He rubbed his chest, still feeling the sting of Kerlvin's claws. He opened his eyes and rubbed them. He rose from the blood-soaked bed. Anger, guilt, loathing, and fear fought for dominance. It was when he was halfway down the hall did he realize his body was still in the bed. His ring was missing. "But it was only a nightmare," he cried.

Three days he waited, three days until someone finally came to find him. They searched the whole house before finally following the smell. The police took one look at the scene. "Yep, looks like they killed each other," stated one officer who was covering his lower face to keep the smell at bay.

"Workers at the mill said they had been arguing," replied another officer. "God, the state of this place. What a dump; not sure if the corpses reek or if it is the house itself."

"What do you expect from rummy?"

"Guess Carl is off the hook." The first cop laughed.

"Yeah, whoever killed him at least tried to make it look like an accident." The first cop shrugged. "Not like this town lost anything with any of these deaths."

"We sure the guy who killed Carl hopped on the first train out of town?"

"Yeah, all covered in blood, the other hobos said. Chattering on and on about a devil taking the soul. The Pittsburgh cops can sort him out."

With little investigation, the police left. Not long after, the grim-faced morticians came to take Edgar's body away. He watched his sheet-covered corpse being loaded into an ambulance. "What good is an ambulance?" he muttered. "I'm already dead." He heard the front door close. He was alone in the house. He had never felt so isolated, so alone. A scurrying scratching of claws told him he wasn't. Back in the room where Edgar had died, Kerlvin sat perched on the end of the bed.

"We'll have a long time together," the demon whispered. "My master did not want your soul." The demon cackled. "Now it belongs to me and this house." His hissing laugh seemed to follow Edgar wherever he went.

Edgar was back within his coils of hate, back in the front room, back listening to the hated voice of the man who had killed him. He could feel it coming. He was ready to commit a true murder. He'd always thought he was a killer; now he was sure of it.

THE DEMON'S REVIVAL

Kerlvin's head was throbbing. It took him several seconds to understand he was lying in the hallway outside Edgar's room. The door lay partially on top of him. There were voices coming up the stairs. He couldn't understand them at first, then the familiar voice of Alex was cut off by another voice. This one he had not heard in many years. This one he hated. An evil grin began to spread across the pointed red face. "Finally," he hissed. The memory flooded back.

Edgar's room darkened as the arch demon sunk slowly back through the portal. Kerlvin was still enjoying the squeaks Edgar made when he walked over the body. He was amused that Edgar thought he still had a body. The crack of light caught Kerlvin's attention. The door stood open barely an inch. The demon approached and listened. A soft "psst" was coming through the opening. Curiosity got the better of him. Suppressing a grin, he moved to throw the door wide open. He could almost hear the crunch of bone and the cries of pain.

Kerlvin stumbled back! His own throat cried out in agony. A hand flew to his left horn; it was missing. Richard's face appeared in the doorway. He held the horn, tapping gently on the tip. "These are very sharp." Richard smiled. "So are those claws," he mused. Anger boiled in the pit of the demon's stomach.

How dare this mortal deprive him of his horn? Kerlvin crouched to spring. The man's blood was already late to stain the walls. Claws scraped wood; wings caught the air in a flutter; the room rushed past. Kerlvin was on his back, lights exploding in his vision.

"Well, well. I guess it is true. You take a bit of a demon..."
Richard casually examined the horn in his hand. "And you are
safe from them. I wonder?" He pointed the horn at Kerlvin.
"You will dance for me."

Despite all his strength and will, the demon danced.
Fighting at every step, he could not throw off the control. He
was able to stop only when Richard said so. Next he found
himself flying in circles around the room. Every time he was
released, Kerlvin tried to attack. After singing, walking
backward, and cleaning the window with his tongue, Kerlvin did
not make an attempt.

"Now, that is a good little demon," Richard cooed at him.
This earned him a snarl but not an attack. "I think you will stay
in this house with my poor departed brother." Richard's
laughing echoed in Kerlvin's pointed ears for hours.

The door flew off, untouched by the demon. He was on his
feet, flexing his four toes. The black claws began to grow sharp
and lethal. His shoulders rolled as the broadened bones cracked
in sequence up his neck, filling the air with gunfire-like
popping. His three-foot frame swelled as strength and power
began to return to his limbs. Kerlvin's wings covered his
shoulders like a cloak. A leather strap appeared across his chest.
A sheath at his hip hung from the strap. He flexed his fingers
while muttering a conjuring spell. With his eyes still closed from
the concentration of the spell, his hand slid down to find the
jewel-encrusted hilt of a short sword. A grin spread across the
thin black lips. His long tail whipped the air with a crack. It
sliced through the thick plaster like it was warm butter. "That
fool brought it with him." Kerlvin's deep growl filled the hall. A
blast of sulfur through a red cloud of smoke left the hall empty.

In the front room, the black cloud darkened and swirled.
Electricity sparked through the bubbling mass illuminating the

sharp-toothed grin and black eyes of Kerlvin, the fifth circle demon. He was a warrior of the legion of Baphoment. Lights in the room faded, drawn into the blackness of hatred, anger, and despair. In the foyer Alex could feel the change creeping in slowly. Behind Richard he could see the lights dimming. As discreetly as he could, he took a step back toward Chloe, reaching back for her hand. Richard was telling a story of an attack on a Korean village. Reveling in the bloodshed, he didn't even notice what was happening around him.

UNEASY PARTNERSHIP

"Hello, old friend." Kerlvin smiled. Edgar spun to face the short demon who had tormented him for years until he got bored. Edgar's fingers traced his cheek as he remembered all the times Kerlvin had shredded it. He could still feel the agony of claws ripping his chest, of the broken ribs from the hopping up and down, claws scratching and ripping with each jump.

Kerlvin had to use those jumping skills as solid black columns of smoke shot toward him. They smashed into the walls as Kerlvin leaped this way and that. He spun in the air, tail flipping. Wings spread, he flew circles over the swirling mass. Changing course, avoiding more lethal spikes, he barely escaped the onslaught. "Relax. I just want to talk," he called. His pause almost cost him his other horn. A blast of electricity singed his cheek. His face distorted in anger. Fire blasted from his hand, parting the smoke on the floor. He caught a glimpse of Edgar before the storm swelled back over him.

"Listen to me!" Kerlvin roared. "Let's kill Richard!" The reply was another onslaught of spikes. Frustration grew as Kerlvin had to continually dodge and weave around the room. Several more failed attempts to strike up a conversation found the creature sitting on the ceiling light. Rage coming out in smoky snorts, a grimace on his face, Kerlvin had had enough. A flash of steel and gold followed by the threshing of wings, he dove into the cloud. The blade struck and clanged against spikes and gauntlets of swirling hate, covering Edgar's arms.

"Would...*you...calm...down...and listen!*" Kerlvin shouted over the cacophony.

"Why should I?" Edgar demanded. "You tortured me!" he lashed out. "I have lived with this guilt!" He ducked a slash from Kerlvin. "You and Richard cursed me to this house." The blade held between two spikes.

"Your bastard brother cursed me to stay here with you." Kerlvin gritted. "I was here to collect your..." Dislodging the sword he parried, spun, holding the blade to Edgar's throat. "Retched soul, not be your babysitter."

Edgar's eyes dared him to do it. "Go on then. Kill me...again." He lifted his head to allow an easier kill. "I never wanted to be here in the first place."

"Your soul is damned and mine." Kerlvin lowered his blade. "I would rather have your brother's."

Edgar took in the lowered weapon and the look on the demon's face. "Do you have a place for him?" he asked. "I know I am going to hell, but is his worse than mine?"

Laughing, Kerlvin threw an arm around Edgar's shoulder. "His pit is lower and full of more torment that you can possibly imagine." He was smiling. "Every death he caused will be dealt back on him. Each death will last centuries. He will feel each lung full of water, every bullet shattering bone, every crushed organ exploding inside the body. Every second will be drawn out and exquisite." Kerlvin was leading Edgar to the French doors. "In fact, I think we may be able to have you assist in punishment."

Edgar shuffled off the demon's arm. "What do you mean?"

Holding Edgar at arm's length, his wings flapping, causing him to move up and down but never breaking eye contact. "You are a being of hatred, anger, and despair." He smiled. "You have everything needed to join us."

"What? Become a demon?"

"Better to be a tormentor than a tormented." Kerlvin shrugged. "Think about it. For now, let's go kill your brother."

"I will. Think about it and kill Richard." Edgar stood in his swirling anger next to the demon. Kerlvin waved his hand. The French doors slowly creaked open. With an evil grin and a nod, Kerlvin bowed to Edgar. Edgar's rage exploded.

Confrontation

Glass shattered, and wood splintered. One door separated from its hinges entirely, exploding onto Richard's back. Alex caught Chloe as she dropped, flinging her clear. Aaron and Arthur dove for cover. Flames shot from Kerlvin's hands while the sword flashed. Lightning and black spears flew from Edgar's cloud, slamming into Richard. He was bent over as bolt after bolt and slash after slash slammed across his back. Alex watched in horror. Richard reached out in front of himself, cracking his knuckles. He rolled his shoulders, cracked his neck, then stood up. Thrusting out a hand, Edgar and Kerlvin flew back into the front room. Stretching his back, Richard slipped a hand into his jacket.

Spitting with anger Kerlvin scrambled forward. Suddenly he stopped, arms outstretched, claws ready to shred, his sword raised to strike. Richard held out the demon's horn. Alex watched as Richard flicked the horn up. Kerlvin flew to the ceiling. Edgar threw stabbing shards of shadow at Richard. They exploded a foot in front of him like he was covered in an invisible dome. Kerlvin fell to the floor. Richard threw out his other hand to block fire from Kerlvin and more spikes from Edgar. Alex's eyes scanned all around, falling on a pry bar lying just the other side of the fight. Throwing himself forward, he ran, then ducked, sliding across the floor. Chloe saw what he was doing and flew at Richard.

Richard had regained control of the demon. He was using him to attack Edgar. Sweat boiled up on his brow. With the fight between Edgar and Kerlvin, Richard lowered his hand, dropping his defense a little. A screaming in his ears and fingers clawed his eyes. Chloe attacked with all she had. She kicked and bit and scratched. Her small fist, holding seventy years of anger, slammed into the side of his head. Richard was more than a match for magical attacks, but the rage of this girl took him by surprise. Instinctively he threw up his arms over his face.

Kerlvin was free. He blasted Richard with a fireball. Richard threw the girl off. He pointed the horn at Kerlvin. Pain exploded in his arm. The horn clattered to the floor. Richard screamed in agony, holding his now-broken arm. Alex's breath was coming in gasps. He held the heavy metal bar like a sword. He was shaking; the snap of the bones still echoed in his ears.

"You will regret that, boy," Richard snarled. A glow showed under the hand holding the broken limb. Richard flexed his fingers. He shook the now-healed arm. Alex saw a flash of silver around Richard's wrist before he was smashed into the wall. The wind knocked out of him, Alex tried to breathe as he tried to pull himself out of the hole he was stuck in. His legs were two feet off the ground. He was bent almost in half, which only compounded his breathing issues. Richard was advancing on him.

"Now you'll feel my true power," he threatened.

At first Richard's smile grew listening to Alex's wheezing attempt to breathe. The smile faltered as the wheezing turned into more of a laugh. Alex forced himself out of the hole. He hit the ground hard. He stayed on his hands and knees for a moment. Spitting blood, he continued to laugh. He forced himself up into a crouched position. His hand on his knees for support and spitting more blood, Alex held out a hand to pause his attacker. Painfully standing up straight, Alex smiled wearily at Richard.

Richard's sneer was back. "Are you ready to die now? Ready to join dear Chloe?"

Staggering a little, Alex wiped his mouth. "I'd be more concerned with yourself at the moment." He laughed, pointing behind Richard.

A soft laughing mixed with heavy angry breathing now reached Richard's ears. Chloe stood there, her eyes ablaze with anger. Next to her was Edgar, his black hatred swirling and crackling with lightning. Finally there was Kerlvin. Slowly he raised his head. Richard took a faltering step back. Kerlvin's twin horns rose gracefully from his head. The ebony shone mirrorlike in the dim light. "So nice to be whole again." The grand demon smiled. "So nice to be in control...again."

"You control nothing," Richard cried, throwing balls of white light at Kerlvin, who flicked them aside lazily. Edgar joined the fight; lighting crashed, strobing the room. In the flash Alex saw the flash of silver again as Richard cast from his left then right then left hand again and again. Edgar and Kerlvin kept up a constant attack. Their advance was slow, but the shield around Richard seemed to be getting closer by the second. Alex waved at Chloe from behind Richard. He pointed at his wrist, then to Richard. Chloe's eyes grew huge. She saw it.

Alex began to edge closer. Richard ignored him. Suddenly Alex stopped and stared. While Kerlvin cackled and sprang into the air flying and throwing flame, Chloe leaned over to speak to Edgar. Shaking his head to clear his confusion, Alex began to move again. Chloe's scream of battle filled the room painfully. Alex caught sight of Aaron and Arthur cowering and covering their ears. Chloe flew at Richard. She was a vision of terror, hair flying, eyes the color of blood, her face gaunt and hollow. She was a specter of pure horror. Richard was stunned by the display. He recovered quickly, waving his hand. She flew against the wall, where she lay stunned.

In the seconds Chloe had distracted Richard, Edgar advanced. The two brothers threw everything they had against each other. Even though Richard was forced back, Edgar was paying a terrible price. Suddenly Edgar's voice cried out from above the fight, "Boy! Grab it!" Alex didn't need an explanation. He took two huge steps and leaped into the fray. Time slowed. Richard cried in triumph as Edgar crumpled to the ground. Kerlvin came in at Richard, sword aimed at his throat. Alex's hands outstretched, his body flying through the air. The small cross stuck into his hand; the chain whipped around his hand as it parted from Richard's arm. Kerlvin's blade slammed into Richard's body. Demon and man fell to the floor. Kerlvin's sword kept Richard pinned to the floor. Blood spurted from his mouth and pooled under him.

"Well, well, well, what shall we do with you?" Kerlvin grinned, tapping his claws on Richard's chest.

Alex got gingerly to his feet. He could feel the thin chain with its tiny charm in his hand. He turned to find Chloe crouched next to Edgar. Alex made his way over on shaking legs. The black cloud was gone now. Edgar seemed small to Alex. "Did you get it?" Edgar whispered.

Holding the chain, Alex let the cross fall from his hand. It swung glinting in the unsteady light from the broken chandelier. "How did you know?" Alex asked but felt he already knew the answer.

"She told me." Edgar gestured weakly to Chloe. He gasped as a tear escaped her eye.

"Thank you, Edgar. I know you didn't kill me, but..." She sniffed. "I forgive you."

Slowly he reached up to grasp her hand. "I know I am going to hell for what I have done." He coughed. "But at least I know I did right by you." Flapping wings and a snicker ruined the moment as Kerlvin arrived.

"I told you I'd have a job waiting for you when we won." Kerlvin beamed. He thrust his hands into Edgar's chest. Edgar screamed in agony. Chloe screamed and clawed at Kerlvin while Alex held her back. Edgar convulsed and contorted, shrinking slightly but growing muscle. His skin turned red while black horns and claws grew. Kerlvin withdrew his hands while Edgar lay breathing heavily. Suddenly Kerlvin stood up, a focused look on his face. "Come on—up. Chop-chop. We have a soul to deal with."

Edgar got slowly to his feet. He regarded Kerlvin for a second, then replied, "Yes, sir."

"You can't take me," Richard spat. "I have a deal with a higher demon than you," he cried as Edgar grabbed his arms. "You can't break the deal."

"Oh dear Richard, didn't you read the fine print? That deal was in place only as long as you had hold of the souls. Since you lost them, you have no deal." Kerlvin's laugh was cruel and malicious.

"No, I still have one. I still have her." As Richard pointed, he saw his naked wrist and the glint from Alex's hand. Kerlvin turned to Chloe and Alex. He smiled an evil grin and was gone in a cloud of sulfur. Edgar kept pulling the screaming Richard, the blade cleaving him as he was dragged to a pit that opened in the floor. The scream was cut off when the hell fires closed. Only the heavy golden sword with its multitude of gems was left behind.

"I think it is over," Chloe said. Before Alex could say a word, she was floating down the hall to the conservatory. Aaron was torn between watching Chloe leave and the golden sword as it teetered and fell heavily to the floor.

FOR HOW LONG?

Alex heard his father and brother speaking softly, then heard the lock click in the front door. He was now alone in the huge old house. Making his way down the hall, his heartbeat increased with every step. She turned to face him as soon as he crossed the threshold. Her sad smile shattered his heart. Chloe was going away soon. There was nothing either could do about that. Edgar was gone. The items taken by his brother had been returned. The other girls had been laid to rest.

Alex's finger ran along the delicate gold chain. He wanted so badly to give it to her. He also wanted nothing more than to keep her with him forever. Her soft words twisted his stomach: "I am bound to this world through that." Her ghostly hand caressed his.

A thought sprang into his clouded brain. "If you are bound to this, and I can take it from the house..." He got lost in thought. *Could it actually work? Would she even want to go?*

Her fingers glided along his face, caressing his cheek. She stroked his furrowed brow. "I think I may be able to leave as well." Her eyes searched his. His hope filled her with its glow. "I would like to go for a walk with you," she whispered.

Alex offered his hand. It was warm and alive to her touch. He could feel her presence yet not really feel her hand in his. It was enough. They proceeded together to the front door. He opened it for her; she smiled her thanks. Each step farther from the house scared her. Each step away also lifted her soul. She was farther away than she had ever been. There was no pain. No pull. Warmth rose from Alex's hand up her arm. The night held a crispness of early spring. She could feel it on her face, a sensation she hadn't known in decades.

Chloe let go of Alex's hand. There was something there. Alex wasn't looking at her. She opened her hand, discovering her necklace. She could feel the ground beneath her feet, the chill on her face. Her coat fluttered as she spun in place. She felt. It was like being alive. Her laughter pieced back together the ragged edges of his torn heart. He turned, not daring to believe. She flew to him, her footsteps clicking along the pavement. She was in his arms laughing.

He buried his face into the rough wool of the coat. Held her along her slender waist and ran a hand along her back. Her arms encircled his shoulders, holding tight. She was standing on her toes. They stayed that way for an eternity or a fleeting second; he was unsure. She relaxed to standing normally. The look on her face as she held on to his upper arms was unreadable. He held her, not willing to let her go. She was there. She was completely there, and she was staring at him with those stunning blue eyes. The world around them blurred and disappeared.

He was lost in those eyes, a sapphire sea as beautiful as the sky and as deep as the ocean. The feelings he held close poured back to him out of those eyes. He inched closer, not knowing what would happen. Her arms moved around his neck as she inched closer to him. She felt so solid in his arms; how long would it last? Could he do this? Her eyes closed slowly, and her head turned slightly. His eyes slid shut. Her lips were warm— her kiss the sweetest. It lasted a few seconds; he didn't want it to end, but he didn't want it to get awkward. She was smiling against his lips. He pulled back, slowly opening one eye.

"I may be the one who hasn't had a kiss in seventy years, but you are the one who needs practice." She laughed, pulling him into a hug. He kissed her again; this one went much better. The night was spent walking through the town. She told him of the past; he told her of the present. Stories were interrupted with the occasional kiss. They walked on as he pushed the nagging question further and further back in his mind: *How long will this last?*